Throw the Amulet

An April May Snow

Southern Paranormal Fiction Thriller

By

M. Scott Swanson

April May Snow Titles

Foolish Aspirations

Foolish Beliefs

Foolish Cravings

Foolish Desires

Foolish Expectations

Foolish Fantasies

Foolish Games

April May Snow Prequel Series

Throw the Amulet
Throw the Bouquet
Throw the Cap
Throw the Dice
Throw the Elbow
Throw the Fastball
Throw the Gauntlet
Throw the Hissy

Never miss an April May Snow release.

Join the reader's club!

www.mscottswanson.com

Copyright © 2022 by M. Scott Swanson

All rights reserved. No part of this book may be reproduced in any form or by any electronic or mechanical means, including information storage and retrieval systems, without written permission from the author, except for the use of brief character dialogue for the purpose of social media memes.

Author's note- This is a work of fiction. Character names, businesses, locations, crime incidents and hauntings are purely imagination. Where the public names of locations are used, please know it is from a place of love and respect from this author. Any resemblance to actual people living or dead or to private events or establishments is entirely coincidental.

Don't throw me no funeral,
Sister don't cry
Saw that fiddle, brother, pass that shine
Deep down in the hollow
Pick the tallest pine
Dig it real deep where the roots touch mine

Whiskey Myers-
"Bury My Bones"

Chapter 1

Unbelievable.

I resist the urge to throw a hissy fit. To prevent me from slinging my phone across the room, I shove it into my back pocket.

The phone call to my *former* best friend, Martin Culp, did not go as I anticipated. Sure, he feels he has a valid excuse since his girlfriend Penny demands he accompany her home to meet her parents.

But the man does not realize meeting the folks is the equivalent of pre-engagement. How he does not comprehend this is beyond me.

Bless it, Sunday is my birthday. My best friend should be here with me, celebrating.

I do a dramatic bellyflop onto my well-worn sofa. Penny tying Martin up all week means I'll be thoroughly bored the entire spring break. I consider the implications of my solitary confinement for the next seven days.

Penny did this on purpose. I have always felt she is uncomfortable that he and I are best friends.

Anyone who knows us understands it was inevitable for us to become the tightest of friends. Martin and I are sports nuts, fantasy nerds, have mean senses of humor, and like to overeat foods that are considered deadly for anyone in the over-fifty age bracket.

Then there is the fact we are both third-year law school students at the University of Alabama. That has compelled us to spend countless hours in one-on-one study sessions.

I think Penny has her knickers in a knot because I'm a girl.

If that is the case, she doesn't understand Martin's relationship with me. It's strictly platonic. Being more than friends with Martin would be like dating one of my brothers. Yuck.

Puffing out my cheeks, I roll onto my back with a dramatic flailing of my arms. It makes me feel better—the drama.

It's not like I don't have other options for spring break. I do. Still, hanging with Martin would be ten times more enjoyable than my other choices. The alternatives to Martin make staying in my apartment by myself and binge-watching *Supernatural* again a really strong option.

There are plenty of my sorority sisters still on campus this week. They would gladly include me in their plans.

But with Susan's wedding scheduled for the end of April, I've already spent too many hours planning the festivities with that group of friends. That is just for the preparation. We'll have countless more hours together with the bachelorette party, rehearsal dinner, and actual wedding.

Thinking of Susan's wedding elicits a groan from me. I'm the coordinator of the bachelorette party. Considering my upcoming forty-eight-hour tour of duty makes my stomach churn. Showing a passel of girls a great time in Nashville and getting them transported safely to the wedding venue in Birmingham is tremendously demanding.

I'm not looking forward to the incredible responsibility. Spending more time with that crowd will only be a constant reminder that the date is "set" and speeding toward me like a freight train.

A road trip to Nashville to visit my cousin Tricia would be enjoyable. But my uncle Norman ruined that idea by planning a family trip to the Science and Industry Museum in Chicago for them this week. He did offer for me to tag along, expenses paid. No, thank you. Not my cup of tea.

I would go home to Guntersville, considering it's my birthday and everything. However, my parents decided this was an excellent week to take the cruise to Belize my daddy has talked about forever. He even convinced Mama to get her scuba diving license.

My parents will be watching colorful fish in crystal-blue water while I'm all alone, turning twenty-six.

I suppose that is what I get for telling them I wasn't coming home for my birthday. Still, it would have been nice if my family made a fuss and insisted I let them give me a party.

I've got to snap out of this. I should consider this a prime opportunity to break in the treadmill I bought myself last Christmas.

Dropping the extra fifteen pounds I've been carrying around would be a worthy project this week. It would guarantee that I won't only dazzle them with my brilliant mind when I start my law career at Master, Lloyd, and Johnson. I'll wow them with my svelte figure, too.

Lifting my hip, I pull my phone out of my back pocket and google "caloric deficit to lose a pound." What? Forget that. I'd need to starve myself for the next two months and walk on my stupid treadmill three hours a day to reach my goal.

It seems like a lot of effort.

Snacking on some potato chips sounds like a much better idea. I roll off the sofa and head for my pantry, debating the positives of Cheetos versus chips and French onion dip.

My phone rings. Thank goodness. That will be Martin coming to his senses. Spending time hanging out with me must be more entertaining than meeting Penny's parents.

Nope. The word *Chase* is displayed on my phone. He is one of my two older brothers. Chase is the younger of the pair—by five minutes—they are fraternal twins.

It's common for him to check up on me every Saturday. Today, being Monday, his call concerns me.

"Is everything okay, Chase?"

"Far from it."

"Oh my gosh." My stomach roils. "What's happened to Mama and Daddy?" I knew their newfound youthful taste for adventure would end badly.

"What? No, they're fine. Mom just sent me a video of their villa a little while ago. Dad did a cannonball off their deck into the ocean. They look like a couple of kids on spring break. "

I calm as I try not to be jealous that I did not receive said video. How difficult would it be for Mama to have included me in the text?

"If they're okay, what is the matter?"

"The Guntersville largemouth bass tourney is this weekend."

Given Chase is an avid angler, I'd think that would be good news for him. The silence hangs far too long for my taste. "And?"

"You know my partner this year, Bryce Cooper, broke his hand while loading pallets down at the dog food factory."

I have no idea who Bryce Cooper is. My family started playing this game when I left for the university. They casually mention somebody's name with an expectant tone as if I know whom they're talking about.

When their silly little game first began, I made the mistake of politely informing them I didn't know the person. This would start a long-winded explanation on their part, attempting to convince me I knew the person in their story. The person I didn't know and didn't care to know. I'm wiser now.

"Yes," I say.

"When Bryce broke his hand, I thought, no problem, I'll get Dad to be my partner."

"He is in Belize," I state the obvious with a tone of bitterness. I'm still sore about not receiving the video from Mama.

"I know. That really blew a hole in that plan."

"Yep."

"Then I thought I'd ask Dusty."

Dusty is the only person in my family who likes freshwater fishing less than me. "Did he say no?"

"No, he agreed to it at first. Then that ex-wife of his messed everything up."

"Bethany?" I pull my phone closer to my ear as I scowl.

"Well, I've got other names for her, but I won't use them in mixed company."

I've got names for her, too. First and foremost, Dusty's biggest mistake.

I reach for the Cheetos on top of my fridge. "If you can't say something nice..."

"Then roll her house."

"But she lives in an apartment with her new boyfriend," I say.

"It was just a metaphor."

I freeze with a Cheeto on my lips, considering if I want to correct Chase about what a metaphor is and determine it would be too much effort. I don't feel like participating in any fool's errands today. I toss the Cheeto in my mouth, crunching it loudly.

"Do you have to eat while you're on the phone?" he asks.

"I'm hungry," I say, emitting a small orange dust storm from my lips.

"You eat more than anyone I know."

"I resemble that remark," I say and grin.

"You need to eat healthier, April."

"I eat healthy."

"You're eating potato chips right now."

My cheeks heat. "I'm eating dried apple chips, if it's any of your business." It's a good thing we are not face to face. It's a fact, I'm the world's worst liar.

"April, you're eating Cheetos."

I check my phone screen to make sure I didn't FaceTime him. I didn't. You can't tell Cheetos by the sound of their crunch. "I am not," I answer him lamely.

"The next time I see you, I will give you a copy of the *Whole Body, Whole Food* book I've been reading. I think it would do you a lot of good."

I'm almost twenty-six years old, and my family thinks I don't have walking-around sense or, in the case of Chase this morning, the ability to eat like an adult. But before my ire can rise, my curiosity is piqued.

Chase reading a book? That's a new one.

"It's a quick read, and the recipes are super easy since it has step-by-step pictures," he adds.

"Oh, it's a cookbook." I stifle a laugh. That mystery was solved quickly.

"Well, yeah. What did you think it was?"

I roll my eyes. "Chase, did you call to critique my diet? Are you that bored?"

"No." He huffs.

"Then why did you call?"

"Well, isn't it obvious?"

I resist banging my head against my refrigerator. Barely. "If I'm having to ask, it's not obvious."

"I need you to fish with me in the tournament this weekend," he says.

My eyebrows shoot into my hairline. "Absolutely not."

"Why not?"

"Because sitting in the middle of the lake, the sun beating down on me, with a major case of swamp butt and second-degree sunburn isn't what I classify as an enjoyable time."

"It's March, April. It's sixty-five degrees and cloudy today."

Fair. "Also, I don't like how fast you drive that stupid bass boat. I'm always coming off the bench seat, and I'm afraid one of these days I'm gonna bounce, catch the wind like a sail, and fly out the back of the boat."

"I guess it's a darn good thing you've been eatin' all those potato chips." He laughs.

He is so stupid. I try not to laugh but fail. "That is not funny."

"I'm sorry. But seriously, help a brother out. You know what this tournament means to me. I also know no matter how much you complain about fishing, you're still three times the fishermen as Dusty."

"I don't complain."

"Yeah, you do. But I block it after a few hours. It's like Charlie Brown's mom. Wa-wa, wa-wa"

"Is your cut down intended to make me want to come help you?"

"No. But I did believe you would want to help your favorite brother out."

I don't have a favorite brother. They are equally aggravating. "I wish I could, but I've got too much going on this week."

"It's your spring break. How can you have too much going on?"

"Believe it or not, Chase, I have a social life. If I'd known earlier, I would, but I've already committed to my friends this week."

The silence is disturbing. An uneasy feeling builds up inside of me, tensing my shoulders. I consider telling Chase I'll do his dopey fishing tournament.

"Okay. I guess it was silly. I'm sorry I put you on the spot."

I exhale in frustration. "It's not like that, Chase."

"Really. No worries. I'll see if Jasper Bell already has a partner. Since I won't see you, happy birthday."

"Thank you."

"Have a fun time with your friends. Love you."

"Okay. Love you, too," I say, then disconnect the call.

I should be relieved. Fishing is not what I want to do this week with my time off.

Instead, I feel guilty and like a lowlife for not helping my brother out.

I pop another Cheeto into my mouth, but I no longer crave them. I clip the bag closed and toss it back on top of the fridge.

The bag hits the Doritos on top of the refrigerator, slides sideways, and falls out of the chip basket. The bag seems to fall in slow motion. The clip comes off as it strikes the floor, and Cheetos scatter across my kitchen linoleum.

Freezing in terror, I watch the last of the orange puffs tumble to a stop. Déjà vu slams into me, stealing my balance. I reach for the counter to steady myself.

I've seen this before.

When I hang up the phone and then spill potato chips,

specifically Cheetos, on the floor, in this exact manner.

That is only the beginning of the extra sight, though. It's not the important part.

In this vision, I'm walking among ancient oaks and cedars. I'm in Guntersville and can see the lake to my left down the hillside. It's evening, and I'm cold. I should have worn a hoodie.

Stabbing pain at the back of my neck forces me to the floor. As I rub the base of my skull, nausea builds in my stomach, and my mouth waters profusely.

Please, no, not this.

I thought I had freed myself of these paranormal events. Freed me of my "gifts," as my grandmothers call them.

I've been kidding myself. Deep down inside, I believe I always knew.

It's true. The regularity of paranormal visions and ghost sightings has diminished exponentially since my first year at college. But never gone entirely.

I still occasionally meet someone for the first time, shake their hand, and know immediately to avoid them in the future. Evil aura stirs up my latent psychic ability.

The random voices from the dead I rarely hear anymore. Still, there is the ghost in the third-floor bedroom at the sorority house. Despite being short on rooms, we use the room as storage space because all the girls can sense something is off with the room. And they are correct.

I pull my knees to my chest and rest my head on my crossed arms. I rock slowly back and forth, willing the memory of the reoccurring vision away.

What had been a vague, foggy dream for the last three nights is now vivid Technicolor in my mind. I don't know why I'm in the woods, but I know it's essential, and I understand my skills are needed there.

Of course, it would have to be Guntersville. All roads dealing with my unnatural paranormal skill set lead back to Guntersville.

It's one of the main reasons I've worked so hard to be able to escape my hometown. Sure, I want to leave to make my mark on the world as the most highly sought defense attorney in the Southeast. I can't do that in a small North Alabama town like Guntersville. But the other aspect is that nowhere else do my "gifts" spike as they do in Guntersville.

Even though they can be aggravating, my brothers are two of my favorite people, and I love my parents dearly. I know I'm blessed to have a loving, supportive family, even if they are too much in my business. But the moment I'm home—even for a few days—strange things happen. It's as if I'm a supernatural magnet. For some reason, Guntersville has a higher level of paranormal activity than most cities.

Sweat beads pop up on the top of my scalp as another flash of migraine pain assaults my neck. I close my eyes and wait for the pain to subside.

Thankfully, the intense pain has made me forget about the need to throw up.

There is no scenario with me returning home this week. Some stupid dream can't compel me to go against my will.

I don't want to fish, and I sure as heck don't want to go traipsing around the woods waiting for a magical vision. Truthfully, I'd rather start that crash diet with the three hours a day on the treadmill than answer my brother's or my dream's request.

But it could be significant. You may be the only one who can help.

"No, no, no!" I bang the back of my head sharply against the cabinet door.

This is so unfair. I simply desire to be normal.

I allow myself a two-minute pity party. It doesn't make me feel any better, only resentful.

Reluctantly, I hit redial. "Hey, Chase. Is that fishing offer still open? I changed my mind."

 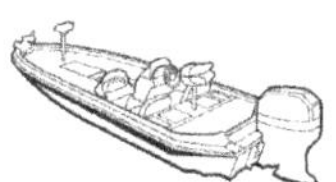 

Chapter 2

Driving up to Guntersville, I'm so mad at myself I could spit. There is no one to blame but myself. It's my fault for not asking for all the particulars about the fishing tournament.

When Chase asked me to participate, I assumed it was a one-day event. As Grandpa Snow used to say, "You make an 'ax' out of you and me when you assume." It was his way to get around putting his dollar in Granny's swear jar that she kept for the fictitious trip to Disney World that never took place.

I understand why Chase is desperate enough to ask me to be his second in the boat. The event is the new Guntersville fishing tourney, where the winner will receive an automatic bid to the Bassmaster Series.

Chase's dream has always been to be a professional bass angler, a NASCAR pit crew member, or a professional football player. If he hadn't started managing the family marina after graduating high school, he was talented and passionate enough to have been a success at any of the three.

Who knows, if he—we—were to win the tournament this weekend, Chase might realize one of his goals. That is extremely cool.

What's not cool is some bozo deciding to make it a three-day tournament. That means three times the misery for April.

As a personal challenge, I promised myself that I would not

complain while we were on the boat. Since learning it is a three-day event, I have abandoned that goal. Even saints have their limits, and I'm no saint.

The event runs Thursday through Saturday. On the positive side, I suppose I'll have Sunday, my birthday, available to drive back to Tuscaloosa. That should make my twenty-sixth birthday the most memorable miserable birthday ever.

Me and my stupid visions. If not for that creepy dream about walking around in the woods, I never would have agreed to this.

Once Chase sent me the text, and I realized it was a Thursday through Saturday event, I should have called him immediately and canceled. Now, Tuesday afternoon, even I know it's entirely too late for Chase to find another partner.

Worse, ever since I agreed to this nonsense, I haven't had the dream. No spilled Cheetos, no cedars and oaks, and no lake. In fact, I haven't dreamed at all since that afternoon that I had the migraine.

Now that I think about it, it probably wasn't a psychic event. It most likely was a simple, good old-fashioned headache. It makes sense. I was stressed out at the time because my plans had gone up in smoke.

After all, because of my careful attention to avoiding places with intense supernatural energies over the last seven years, I know my "gifts" have atrophied. So why did I assume this was a paranormal call to return home?

Because I insist on overthinking everything. One of these days, I'll learn that most things in life are random, and contrary to what some people say, things don't always happen for a reason.

Oh well, I'm committed now. As much as Chase did for me when I was in middle school and high school, I suppose I can suck it up for a few days and be the supportive sister I want to be.

It's not gonna kill me to do my brother a favor. I will smile and be a big girl because supporting each other is what a family does.

But I won't lie. I'm dreading three days discussing whether I should use spinnerbait or purple worms, and if I'm jigging the line correctly as I'm reeling it in. I'm sure he only means to be helpful. He can't help but constantly critique my form and bait selection.

I clear Malfunction Junction in Birmingham and take the Tarrant exit off Interstate 59. State Highway 79 is not the shortest route to Guntersville. But I feel a bit nostalgic and want to see if there have been any developments in the area I once knew so well.

There have been a lot of nostalgic moments in my life lately. That and brutal prioritization of what is essential in my life.

I'm sure it has to do with the impending completion of my law degree and the start of my "real" life. Soon I will be on my own in a demanding career path. I am anxious to step into my career and understand that it will be all-consuming.

I did not make my career choice randomly. I am fortunate enough to have an uncle who is an attorney. My daddy's older brother, Howard, is an attorney in Guntersville.

In some ways, I followed in his footsteps. He is a University of Alabama law school graduate. The only difference between us is he always intended to move back home once he passed the bar and help the people of Marshall County.

His decision is admirable, but my law degree took entirely too much effort to waste on small-town cases. Not to mention I have so much student debt now that I must make the big bucks, and quickly.

Tarrant looks even longer in the tooth than I remembered. Many of the old industrial facilities are shuttered now. The backside of Center Point coming up on Jefferson State, locally referred to as Harvard on the Hill, is looking rougher than I remember.

As I turn right and head up the knoll toward Pinson, I see the other reason I came this way. I pull into the parking lot of Connie's Confectionery Castle.

Susan's dad insisted she order her wedding cake from Connie's. Connie is the daughter of a condominium developer who contracts most of his concrete from Susan's dad.

Understandably, Susan is worried about whether this bakery can handle the job. Truthfully, Susan stresses over everything. I love her, but she is about on my last nerve, and she is a frog's hair away from being the stereotypical bridezilla. This is even worse in her case because she is usually such a sweet girl.

Stepping inside, sugar and vanilla envelop me. I close my eyes as the bell tingles behind me. If I were to die right now, I would die happy. The only thing better would be to have a cupcake in my hand.

The ambiance of the store charms me into a grin. It's not the sugar talking to me. The buoyant energy of creativity and love inside the establishment caresses me, causing my skin to tingle.

"Can I help you?"

I smile so broadly I feel my face stretch. "Hi, I'm helping a friend plan a wedding, and I was curious if y'all make wedding cakes?" Susan's dad has already ordered the cake. My mission is to go incognito and check Connie's out for Susan.

I'm incredibly pleased and relieved as I get back on Highway 79.

My covert mission was a smashing success. Connie showed me an extensive portfolio of wedding cakes from her other weddings.

Most importantly, she had the product for me to taste test, including the lemon cake Susan's dad ordered. My sweet tooth was enthralled by the delicate taste.

Not only does Connie create magical cakes, but she is also one heck of a salesperson. I don't know if she assumed by my curves that I am an avid cupcake eater or if it is how she usually seals the deal. Regardless, I have a complimentary four-pack of beautiful cupcakes riding on my passenger seat.

It is almost enough to make me want to marry someone, just so I can order one of her wedding cakes. Almost.

I dial Susan's number. "Hey, I want to let you know I checked out that bakeshop."

She exhales rudely. "Is it awful?"

"The worst. It has a health rating of seventy-four, and all the help smokes. It was like walking into a fog bank when I opened the door to their shop. How did your dad find this dive?"

"I knew it. I'm gonna kill my dad."

I intended to tease her more, but she sounds homicidal, and her dad is a nice enough fellow. "Don't go off halfcocked. I was just kidding you."

"April! That is not even funny."

"It's a little funny."

"Stop it. Tell me the truth."

"The truth? You need to give your dad a big hug the next time you see him. This place is a winner."

Another rush of air from Susan. "Oh, thank goodness. That is such a relief, April. Thank you for going behind his back and checking it out for me."

"No worries." I wasn't about to mention the free cupcakes even though I'm tempted to. In Susan's present state, she will think that had something to do with my glowing review. I had already decided about the bakery before anyone offered a cupcake bribe.

"Is everything taken care of for the bachelorette party?"

"What's the point of having me plan the festivities if you're going to worry about it?"

My phone emits a dreadful siren. I look at the screen to see what the warning is.

"What is that noise?"

I read the text. My skin tingles like a thousand ants with whiskered legs are crawling across my neck. The sensation makes me shiver. "It's an Amber alert."

"Oh, I hate those," Susan says.

"Hopefully, it'll have a happy ending."

"I hope so." Susan clears her throat. "But everything is good on the bachelorette party in Nashville?"

"I've got it. You just need to show up and quit worrying about it."

"Okay. I'll do my best."

I laugh because I know she won't quit fretting about it until it's over. "Thank you. I'll see you next week."

"No, thank you. I appreciate everything you're doing for me, April."

"My pleasure."

I tap open the Amber alert again after I disconnect from Susan. Something about it gives me the heebie-jeebies. Jaxx Dolin, age five, was last seen in Arab, Alabama. Short blond hair, blue eyes, forty-four inches tall, and forty-five pounds.

When I turn onto State Highway 75 toward Guntersville, I'll drive right by Arab.

An uneasiness builds in my gut. It's nearly enough to knock the shine off of getting four free cupcakes.

I try my best not to focus on the alert. It's not like I can do anything about it anyway. Unless I were to see an average-sized five-year-old wandering along the side of the road, whatever a five-year-old looks like.

The police probably already have this under control. How often have I seen an Amber alert and then found out that the child has already been returned safely to their parent the following day?

Most alerts describe the vehicle the child is traveling in, or sometimes the clothes the child is wearing or even the adult they may be traveling with. Other than the basic description a pediatrician could give the police, this alert is scant on any real clues.

That is disconcerting.

I attempt to push my feelings about the emergency of the Dolin child further out of my mind. I'm sure he wandered off into the woods behind his house, and the adults will find him soon.

As it is, I have more on my plate than I can say grace over. Completion of the last few assignments, including one final mock litigation before earning my juris doctorate and keeping my former pledge Susan Esposito from driving me and all of her friends crazy before she marries Jackson Taylor next month. A man, oddly, few of us have met yet.

My left eyelid twitches uncontrollably. I close that eye to make it stop, but it continues to pulsate.

Quickly, I pull my sunglasses off my face and toss them onto the passenger seat. I place the palm of my left hand firmly against my eye, hoping it will cease the spasming muscle.

It aggravates the stew out of me when this happens. When I was younger, it happened all the time.

If I became agitated over a test that I hadn't studied for or if I talked to a boy I had a secret crush on—bam—uncontrollable eye twitch. Always it was only my left eye. It made it difficult on exams I wasn't prepared for, not to mention it wasn't the best look when talking to a boy I wanted to impress.

No wonder I am being afflicted with this odd malady, considering the level of tension I'm feeling today. It's Chase's fault. His dopey bass tournament and his need to scope out the lake the day before the competition.

A lake he has lived on his entire life. Like he will find some new hot fishing hole to fish today. And as if I might be able to help in that venture.

That is probably what is causing this stupid eye twitch. That and being almost home to Guntersville.

Coming around a bend of pine trees, as I approach a narrow bridge crossing one of the many small inlets, a fast-approaching red blur appears in my lane. I squint my right eye attempting to bring it into focus.

I drop my left hand from my twitching eye in hopes of improving my depth perception as my jaw drops open. A crimson pickup truck is in my lane, attempting to pass several cars.

My fingernails bite into my palms. The truck will not clear the cars in time.

There is no room for evasive maneuvers since I'm already on the bridge. With no shoulder available for me to utilize to give the truck more space, all I can do is brake and pray.

Time slows. The color leeches from my vision, and I see only monotone as I grit my teeth and hug the right-side curb.

The nose of the truck lifts, and a black puff of diesel smoke trails behind the truck as he speeds up. All the laws of momentum, learned by the daughter of a physicist, run through my head. I'm nearly stopped in a subcompact vehicle. The oversized truck is moving at eighty miles an hour.

I'm about to die.

Please, no. Not yet.

For a second, frozen in time, the glare from the sun disappears from the truck windshield, and we are lined up face to face. Sandy blond hair, short on the sides, full-bearded jaw, eyes narrowed in desperate determination. I wonder if he can see me as clearly. If he sees my fear.

The driver's hands jerk to the right. His truck responds by squatting to the right as it slides into the correct lane, threatening to lift two of its tires. It's inconceivable how we don't collide.

Three cars are lined up behind me in my rearview mirror, waiting patiently. I sit at a dead stop, no pun intended, on the state highway. Feeling uneasy about driving, I press the accelerator cautiously so I don't hold up the people behind me longer than necessary. I don't want to avoid one accident only to be the cause of someone else getting rear-ended.

It's just beyond me how ignorant some drivers are. They are willing to kill someone else in a head-on collision to get to wherever they're going a few seconds early. Half the time, with these state highways, when you pass somebody, they pull up right behind you at the next red light. Making it clear what a jerk you were for endangering everyone.

The ringing of my phone startles me from my thoughts.

It's Chase, which irritates me. "I swear, Chase. You are as persnickety about punctuality as Mama. I told you I'd be there by one, and I'll be there at one." Or 1:15. After that near-miss accident, I have the urge to pee. On the positive, my stupid left eye has grown tired of twitching.

"April," Chase says in his calm voice, which often signifies a forthcoming session of mansplaining.

"You know, if you're that eager to scout out the lake, just go ahead without me. It's not like I can help."

"April, forget about the boat trip for a second."

My mouth snaps shut as I realize something besides my tardiness has Chase upset.

He makes a clicking noise with his tongue. In my mind, I see him running his hands through his hair.

"Did you get an Amber alert a few minutes ago?"

The oddity of the question fills me with dread. "Yeah."

Chase clears his throat. "I don't know a good way to tell you. But I think you know her."

I squint my eyes. Realizing it's as much for me trying to make sense of Chase as it is the bright sun assaulting my eyes. I reach over to the passenger seat, attempting to retrieve my sunglasses. "There must've been two alerts, and we got different ones, Chase. The one I saw was for a little boy."

"Right. Jaxx Nolin. You knew his mother."

Chapter 3

My stomach tenses from an overwhelming sense of dread. Still, I don't know any Nolins. Chase must be mistaken about the child's mother being a friend of mine. "I don't know anybody named Nolin."

"I'm afraid you do."

I settle in for a long-winded story where Chase will attempt to convince me how I know this child's parents. I suppose it won't hurt me to play along and act like I know them, and then express the requisite amount of concern for the return of their little boy. I may not be an acquaintance of the parents, but Chase is. A little white lie on my part would help move us off the unpleasant topic and soothe my brother's mind. "How so?"

"Gemma Kruse was Jaxx's mother."

It starts at the base of my neck. The cold chill of trepidation radiates across my shoulders. Gemma Kruse and I were, indeed, friends once.

Gemma and I were in the same grade at Guntersville High School. She didn't start there. Her mom moved her and her younger sister to town at the beginning of Gemma's sophomore year.

I've been privileged. Despite Daddy having multiple job promotion offers that would have required relocating our family, Mama never allowed him to consider moving us. The only move I knew was in seventh grade when my parents bought their "forever" home on Lake Guntersville. It was only a two-mile trek across town, and I remained in the same school. We moved everything as a family project that took an entire week. I was rewarded with a massive bedroom with a lakeside view for my hard work. There was nothing to complain about.

The point is, I never experienced being the new kid in school. Frankly, until Gemma, I never really considered how difficult it was for the students whose parents decided to drop them into our school system. At our school, we knew so much about the other families that we felt related even when we weren't.

Anyone new was decidedly an outsider.

Even more unfortunate for Gemma, it was apparent from the outset that she was from little means. So many of the Guntersville crowd, who are less fortunate than my family, fought hard to keep up airs of prosperity. Which often led to families fracturing under the stress of untenable credit card debt and mortgages that left them perpetually teetering on the brink of financial ruin.

In some twisted manner, it gave those girls the perceived right to incessantly pick on anyone who didn't have the right shoes, their own car, or manicures. They were at the top of the food chain. To retain their superiority, it was necessary to keep any new potential usurper ostracized and demoralized.

I never participated in the teasing, but not because I'm a person of virtue. I mainly found it odd to be picking on people I didn't know. In retrospect, given my strong influence in the groups I ran in, solely by virtue of my parents' affluence, I wish I had shut it down. And I could have without a word spoken. A stern look would have done the trick.

There is nothing to be done about it now. Opportunity missed. Back then, I didn't understand the dynamics of what was going on around me. I only knew it made me uncomfortable.

At five foot nine, Gemma was as tall as me. But the similarities ended there.

Gemma was long and wiry, whereas I have had significant

curves since I was fifteen. She had a masculine gait, and with her home-cut red hair and loose-fitting no-name blue jeans, it was easy to mistake her for a prepubescent boy from behind. Her face, bleached-white flour speckled with chocolate freckles across her nose, couldn't be considered pretty.

Knowing the deck was stacked against her, her crystal blue eyes were always alert and scanning the room. More predatory than prey, they hardened her features, further making her even less attractive if that were possible.

It was a face I would come to love over the next three years. Never my best friend; that would have been too difficult for us. She was someone I trusted implicitly because I knew her drive and strength was equal to mine, and we shared a common goal. To escape Guntersville, Alabama.

Ten weeks after coming to Guntersville High School, Gemma had the audacity to show up for cheerleading tryouts. Our school held cheerleader tryouts twice a year—in the fall for the basketball squad and spring for next year's football squad. The squad lineup only changed for two reasons. A girl quit, which only happened in the case of a great scandal. Or a member moved out of town, which was an even rarer occurrence.

Still, several girls would always show up and try to unseat one of the current team members. Understandably, because of the reality of a limited squad, the current cheerleaders were never in a helpful mood for the girls trying out.

Despite what you're probably thinking, the most significant limitation for the newcomers wasn't political, socioeconomic, or the preference of coach Judy Mizner. A former college gymnast, Coach Judy had a high propensity to believe cheerleading was more about dazzling gymnastic stunts than chanting cheers. Consequently, she would cut any girls who fell short of her gymnastic requirements.

I come from a lengthy line of people whose last words before a visit to the emergency room are, "Hey, y'all, watch this." Consequently, I've never had an issue with back handsprings, flips, or aerial cartwheels. But I am the exception to the rule, at least in Guntersville. Every year we would have a few girls on the squad terrified of the stunts required during our exhibitions.

Girls would spend countless hours practicing with spotters, and their parents paid vast sums of money to professional cheerleading coaches. And still, when it came time to perform, they would become scared and fail spectacularly. They would mess up the mechanics of their back handspring, causing them to sprain an ankle or land awkwardly, pushing them forward into a face plant on the hardwood floor.

Not Gemma. She was fearless.

During that tryout, when she was still an outsider to the school, she drew the unenviable task of going first for the gymnastic portion of the tryout. For the first time in my many years of cheerleading, I felt the competitive fire stoke in my belly. I watched her snap off a back handspring and plant a perfect landing without hesitation, and I knew it was better than mine. For the first time, I had competition.

When I saw her complete a round off back handspring and follow it up with the most exquisitely performed aerial cartwheel I have ever seen, I knew I was no competition to her.

Coach Judy was equally awed. We both knew we were watching something special.

Lana Hardy was the only returning cheerleader who did not make the team. Considering she had suffered three concussions the prior year due to nasty falls, she appeared relieved when the last name called was Gemma.

Gemma's. Mrs. Hardy did not accept defeat so graciously. She took it up with the principal the next day. Principal Eaves declined to get involved in the decision, in typical male fashion.

For her part, Gemma appeared shocked when her name was called. Standing to the side of the group, she remained frozen as she stared at Coach Judy.

No one moved to congratulate the last addition to our team. Everyone else's name had been greeted by squeals of excitement and numerous hugs.

The awkward silence hung in the air. I finally decided that the responsibility fell to me since I was the freshman squad captain. To get to Gemma, I was forced to walk across the front of my teammates and failed contestants. Gemma didn't come across as a hugger, so I stuck out my hand.

"Congratulations, Gemma. Welcome to the team," I said.

She fixed her crystal blue eyes, shining with tears, onto me. "She is letting me on the team?"

It was such a preposterous statement I had to stifle a laugh. "No. You earned your way onto the team. We're lucky to have you."

That was the first time any of us had seen Gemma smile. I drew back, surprised by the sight of the unfortunate gap between her two front teeth. A gap wider than a number two pencil.

Something about her made me love her. I think it was that she was just real. Something I have sought to be, as I go through life, often feeling like a fraud and never being sure exactly who I am.

Later, when I asked, Gemma explained that her goal was to get a cheerleading scholarship to afford college. It was the only way that she saw she would be able to attend since her mom was struggling to keep the rent paid on the three-bedroom house they lived in out by the dog food factory.

She wanted to be an engineer. Math, chemistry, and physics came easy to her, as they did to me.

Gemma never minded that the other girls kidded her about being a science brainiac. She also never outed me as a fellow science nerd.

Sadly, she didn't earn that cheerleading scholarship. Come to find out, they're incredibly competitive, and few are handed out to students who aren't already on campus.

By then, I had learned that Gemma's daddy had died during Operation Enduring Freedom in Afghanistan. He was a Marine and was posthumously awarded the Bronze Star. Even at eighteen, the irony did not elude me. Her father fighting for our country's freedom had devastated his family's future.

It didn't seem fair.

It did explain a lot about my friend to me. She was her father's daughter. A fighter.

As I was heading off to Alabama, compliments of my parents, I remember the last night we talked. I was trying to convince her that she should follow me to Alabama and that she would figure out a way to make it work the way she always had everything else. She would get that cheerleading scholarship she needed if she was on campus.

Instead, she insisted that she stay in Guntersville and attend community college and then maybe transfer to the University of Alabama Huntsville if things were better in a couple of years. I couldn't comprehend what she was saying. For the first time ever, the fearless Gemma said something she wanted couldn't be done.

In retrospect, it was a solid plan. But I didn't think it was good enough for someone as bright and talented as Gemma, and I continued to argue, saying, "It's not like you to be afraid." That is on me.

"April, you just don't get it. You've gone through life with everybody taking care of you and every door opened to you. But we're not all like you. Some of us must take care of other people and other things. We don't all get to go through life being the princess!" She blew up on me.

Her words stung me to the core. The friend I welcomed into my group the last three years, the one I had been sure to include in everything, had turned on me and belittled my very existence.

With tears forming in my eyes, I choked out the words, "If that's how you feel." I got in my car and struggled to drive home through my blurred vision as the tears streamed freely.

The following year, by a chance meeting with a fellow Guntersville High School graduate, I learned of Gemma's mom's death. Ms. Kruse had died of an accidental overdose. The friend informed me it had been an issue ever since her husband had died, and it had become progressively worse.

At that moment, I realized Gemma stayed behind as much to take care of her younger sister and mom as anything else. As it turned out, Gemma wasn't afraid. She was being as brave as ever.

I wanted to call her, but her mother had died seven weeks earlier from what the person told me. It seemed too awkward to reach out so belatedly. If I were as brave as her, I would have called and admitted that I had been wrong the year before.

It's been seven and a half years since we last talked. I'm sure that is my loss.

"April, do you remember Gemma?"

My brother's voice brings me back to the present, and I try to sound normal to cover the shame I feel. "Yes. She was a good friend to me in high school."

"I thought so."

"I just knew I didn't know any Nolins."

"You might not have. Stephen Nolin was two years older than Dusty and me. When you started, he would've already been out of school."

"Psycho Stevie?"

"You know him?"

"Yes, he bussed tables at the Landing for a while."

"Yeah, I think you're right," Chase agrees.

"I know I'm right. Our senior year, Jackie Rains and I used to go to the Landing on Saturday afternoons for their hamburger special. This guy with a name tag, Stephen, would always come into our section after we sat down and hung around doing busy work while we ate. Every time we looked up, he would be gawking at us."

"Why didn't you leave?" Chase scolds.

"Well, first off, the Landing burgers are great at full price, but you can't turn them down at half price before noon. Second, we thought he was harmless. Maybe a little psycho given his crazy eyes, hence 'Psycho Stevie.' But it didn't seem like that big of a deal until the time he propositioned us for a ménages à trois."

"You're kidding. What were you, like, seventeen at the time?"

"Just."

"I'll kill the pervert if I ever see him. Why didn't you tell me?"

"Uh, because of that."

"That, what?"

"I don't want you going to jail for killing some dumb guy. Besides, we just quit going to the Landing. He probably did us both a favor as the habit was beginning to grow on my hips, if you know what I'm saying."

"I don't see how you can be so glib about this."

"Oh, stop it, Captain America. Contrary to your belief, I have been capable of taking care of myself for a long time now."

"The jury is still out on that."

I snort. "Sure, whatever." It occurs to me that if I brag to my brother about being able to take care of myself and being brave, it would be an excellent time to demonstrate that. Sure, there is no doubt it will be awkward calling Gemma after all these years, but I'm sure she is scared right now, and even though she still has her sister, I bet she could use someone else to talk to, too. Even if it is a friend who disappeared like a ghost, years earlier. "Do you happen to have her number? I feel like I need to give her a call."

Chase remains silent for too long, making me think that we dropped our connection. "Chase? Are you there?"

"Yeah, I'm still here."

"If you don't have it, just let me know. Seeing as you've been so kind as to notify me of my friend's new last name, I can Google her information when I stop," I joke.

"You can't," he whispers gravely.

I roll my eyes. Before I can come back with something witty to say, Chase cuts me off.

"April, Gemma is dead."

Chapter 4

The air rushes out of my lungs, leaving me gasping. I either misunderstand my brother, or he is playing another one of his unfunny sophomoric jokes. "That's not humorous, Chase. It's actually sort of sick."

"I know it's terrible to have to have this conversation on the phone. I wanted to wait to tell you—until you arrived at the lake house. But with the Amber alert going off, I didn't want you to figure it out on your own. I really am sorry, April."

I didn't think this conversation could make me feel any more ashamed than it already had, yet here we are. For the first time in my life, I wish a family member wouldn't believe I am smart. I'm confident that I would never have put together Gemma with the missing child alert.

My nose tingles wildly as tears well up in my eyes. My throat has constricted so tightly that it is challenging to ask, "Today?" As if it would make a difference when she died.

"Yeah. Whoever took Jaxx ran into a very protective mama bear. The boys said that by the looks of the place, she gave the intruder an epic fight."

Of course, she would have. I wouldn't expect anything less from Gemma. Still, it doesn't ease the pain in my chest. In fact, I don't care to know any more of the details.

"I'm gonna let you go, Chase."

"Hey, wait. How far out are you? I want to know that you're okay."

I draw in a deep breath, hoping that it will loosen my throat so that I don't sound like I'm on the verge of hysteria, although I am. "I'm only twenty minutes away."

"Are you okay? I mean, I know you're not *okay*, but you're safe to drive?"

Even though he can't see me, I nod. "I'll be fine. I'll see you in a few."

"I'm really sorry, April."

"I know. I'm glad you told me." I don't think I am, but there is no use in him feeling lousy for being brave enough to break the shocking news to me.

I disconnect the line and turn the radio off. The pine forest blurs on either side, occasionally giving way to a small water inlet before returning to the forest.

Struggling to keep the tears at bay, I concentrate on Gemma's son and tell myself that at least there is a part of her that will continue. In my heart, I know they will find her boy and return him to his aunt.

It'll be hard for him at first, but plenty of kids are raised by their extended family members. The thought does little to cheer me, and I pull in front of a convenience store.

Wandering like a zombie, I make my way into the store. I have a singular mission to find milk.

The perfect thing to hold the blues at bay is copious amounts of sugar. How fortunate for me that Connie gifted me four beautiful cupcakes. All I need now is milk.

It hasn't even been ten minutes since Chase gave me the awful news. I've already tried and convicted myself for the murder of Gemma. I don't know if she was stabbed, shot, choked, or thrown down the stairs, but it doesn't matter. I'm still the guilty party.

You think I'm exaggerating, but it's a true story.

If I had stayed in contact with Gemma, I would have learned that she was going out with Psycho Stevie. She would still be alive if I had warned her what a creeper he is.

It is a tremendous burden to carry.

I struggle to get the four-pack cupcake clamshell open. My frustration peaks as I can't figure out the clear lid to the point I believe the waterworks will begin again. The plastic cover magically pops open, and the cab of my car fills with the scent of sugar and vanilla as I greedily grab a white frosted cupcake.

Hurriedly, I clamp my teeth down on the sweet treat, and my tongue comes in contact with something foreign. Opening my mouth wide to remove the cupcake, I wonder if this trip can get any worse than it already is. Even my free cupcakes are jacked.

Nope. On closer inspection, the cupcake is perfect, but I'm an idiot. It is still customary to remove the wrapper before eating cupcakes.

If there were a competition for cupcake speed eating today, I would be the champion. The digital clock in my dash doesn't have time to change one digit before the white cupcake has disappeared and relocated into my tummy.

I pull the safety ring from the milk container, pop the top, and take a swig in one swift motion. Swallowing the milk tinged with the remaining sugar, my shoulders relax. I slouch into my pleather bucket seat.

There is nothing I can do about Gemma. It's one of those unfortunate events that happen even though you wish it didn't. Still, in the end, what is done is done, and there is nothing I can do that will bring Gemma back. My time to help her has come and gone. As much as I may hate that I missed my opportunity.

Looking down, I'm surprised a second cupcake has disappeared. I seriously consider eating a third but decide the mature thing to do is share the rest of my treasures with my two brothers.

I finish off the milk and throw away the wrapper and container. The day has gone from frustrating to devastating. Either way, I still have to get through it. I start my car to finish the last ten minutes of the drive to my parents' house.

The shock of my friend's death settles in, and my overactive curiosity whirls into high gear in my head. I have so many questions: who attacked her, why were they after Jaxx, and yes, even the morbid detail of how did she die?

I know that the police are diligently working on the first two questions. The last, how Gemma died, I would be better off never learning. Having the visual of my friend's death stuck in my brain for the next few years couldn't do me any good.

Yes, the best thing for my sanity is to push her death as far from my mind as possible. I'll say a prayer for Gemma tonight, but otherwise, I can't allow myself to fixate on the tragedy. Because I can't affect it.

I flip the radio back on in hopes that it will offer some diversion. I listen to each station for three seconds before pushing the button to move to the next channel.

Why didn't the police describe who took Jaxx and what they were driving? Does that mean that nobody saw Jaxx taken from his home?

If Gemma put up such a fight as Chase described, surely a neighbor heard the commotion. Where are all your nosy neighbors when you need them?

"Ugh." I slam my head against my headrest in frustration. I'm doing exactly what I said I wouldn't do—think about Gemma's death.

A friend who stayed in touch with Gemma might have reasonable cause to fixate on her murder. Heck, a good friend might have enough decent information to develop a hypothesis. Instead, I'm an outsider in her life. I left her in my rearview mirror like some anonymous mile marker I passed earlier in my life.

Too abruptly, I step on the brakes and swing my car into the left median. I nearly missed the turnoff to my parents' neighborhood during my self-loathing session.

Taking a left, I cross the traffic on the state highway safely. I turn right as I pass Bill's Bait and Fuel.

I must really be upset. Typically, I'm on autopilot driving to my parents' home. And yet today, I almost missed the turnoff.

Turning into the lake house driveway, I get another shock. It seems today is just full of surprises.

One of Chase's reasons for me coming home to do the fishing tournament with him was that my other brother, his fraternal twin Dusty, wouldn't be in town. But I'm looking at Dusty's immaculately refurbished '67 GTO next to Chase's jacked-up 4 x 4 Silverado.

So help me, if Chase made me drag myself up here because Dusty didn't *want* to go fishing, he will be sorry. No. They will both be sorry.

I don't even bother to grab my backpack when getting out of my car. I slam my car door and stomp onto the back porch toward the sliding glass door entry into the kitchen.

I'm not sure whom I'm going to give a piece of my mind to yet, but I know I'm loaded for bear, and somebody better do some quick explaining.

My thunder is stolen as the glass door slides open and Dusty steps out. The look of alarm on his face makes me stop in my tracks.

He has the element of surprise, and it temporarily freezes me. Which prevents me from escaping his hug.

"I'm so sorry, April," he says over my head and crushes me to his chest.

I squirm and push against him. Dusty is a huge guy, and it's like being hugged by a bear.

"I thought you weren't going to be here." It pops out of me, sounding more like an accusation than a question.

"It's important I be with you."

Be with me? It seems like an overreaction for my brothers to think I need so much consoling. Maybe I should let them in on what a poor friend I was to Gemma the last seven years so they can be ashamed of me, too.

Before I can say anything to Dusty, Chase comes out of the sliding glass door, turns, and locks it. "Are you ready to go?" Chase asks.

"I just got here."

"I'm glad you made it safe." Chase pats my shoulder as he passes by me. "Let's saddle up."

Dude, it's like constant mental wind sprints around my brothers. "Where are y'all going? And how about you unlock the door for me?"

Dusty studies me as he grabs his red beard. It desperately needs to be trimmed. "To your friend's house."

I give him my much-practiced "you've got to be kidding me" expression.

"To see if you get any visions that might be helpful," Dusty explains.

"Come on, folks. Before we lose any more daylight," Chase says as he climbs into his truck.

Dusty appears to understand that I am not comprehending. He is smart like that. He makes a circular motion with his hand.

I'm distracted by the new tattoo he has added to his right arm. It nearly completes his ink sleeve on that side.

"Your gift. I figure you will want to try and see who kidnapped Jaxx to save him."

My expression doesn't change. I add a shake of the head for punctuation. "No."

"No?"

I don't mean to be rude, but I grunt inadvertently. "What would give you that idea?"

"I figured you would want to help. Jaxx is only a kid."

"I get that, and I wouldn't mind helping. But I don't think my gifts will help the situation."

"Sure, they would. If we knew who took Jaxx, we could whittle down where we need to check for him."

I try to push past Dusty toward the glass door. "No. Absolutely not."

"He is just a little boy, April."

I reach the glass door. Having already forgotten that it's locked, I give it a tug that nearly pulls my fingertips off. I pivot and glare at my brothers. They both watch me intently. The look of expectation in their eyes makes me groan.

"I don't have the psychic abilities anymore," I say as I stomp my foot.

Chase, standing between the driver's door and the cab of his truck, looks down from his perch. He resembles a dressed-down male model with his sandy-blond hair and tan. "Come on, April. A little boy's life is at stake."

"I heard you two the first time. What exactly are y'all expecting me to do?"

Chase points at Dusty as he says, "You know, that mumbo-jumbo stuff that Dusty always says you can do."

Chase has never displayed a hint of psychic ability. In Chase's world, if he can't do it, it doesn't exist.

Dusty, on the other hand, occasionally exhibits some minor capabilities. At best, he has one percent of my paranormal abilities. I suspect we might be on equal par now that my skills have atrophied.

"Guys, I would love to help, but I don't have the gift anymore. I haven't used it in seven years, and it's just gone away." To emphasize it, I pass my right hand in front of me flat, signifying something going by.

Dusty laughs. "Skill like yours doesn't go away."

"Well, it has," I challenge.

"April, Officer Slater didn't want to give me access to the house initially. If you don't go now, you won't ever get the opportunity again." Chase points at me to emphasize. "If I know you, weeks, months, even years from now, you'll wonder if you could have made a difference."

Chase isn't book smart like Dusty and me. Still, I must give the boy credit. His logic is always flawless.

He is correct. If I don't go, I will always wonder if something would have triggered in my mind and helped the situation. Information that will find Gemma's killer, bring him to justice, and save her son.

The trouble is, my brothers will expect results. Results that I already know I can't deliver.

With both staring at me, I know I don't really have a choice.

"I guess it couldn't hurt," I say as I make my way to the truck.

"Thatta girl. You won't regret this," Chase says.

I contemplate hopping up and taking the shotgun position in the truck. Instead, I duck onto the back bench seat of the cab, so Dusty won't have to fold his six-five, three-hundred-twenty-pound frame into the back of the truck.

As we pull out of the driveway, I attempt to manage their expectations one last time. "Y'all don't understand. Because I haven't been using my gifts, they have all but disappeared. Please don't be disappointed if I'm not able to help."

"You'll be great," Dusty says.

Dusty thinks the psychic abilities are something I can turn on and off at will. I wish that were the case. It would be wonderful to have that level of control over them. Instead, they are much more random.

"The important thing is that you tried and did everything you could," Chase says.

After a few minutes, Chase pulls up to a curb. I look out my window as my brothers open their doors simultaneously.

"This is it?" I ask.

It's a silly question—given the Boaz police cruiser in the driveway and the yellow caution tape across the front porch columns—and it's one Chase graciously ignores.

"Oh, good. Buzz is still here. Maybe he has some more information."

I exit Chase's truck and stare in disbelief at the home where my friend met her end.

 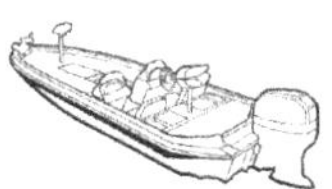 

Chapter 5

Gemma and I often discussed what sort of home we wanted to live in when we grew up. She had what I felt was an odd fascination with the colonial style.

When we would have these talks, my dream home changed every conversation. Once, it would be a lake house like my parents, but obviously not in Guntersville. Then the next time, it might be a high-rise condominium in Miami.

Gemma's dream home always remained constant. A two-story colonial style, with not four but six columns on the front porch, is what she wished for. As a bittersweet emotion washes over me, I admire the beautiful gray brick of the impressive home. I'm confident I'll find a swimming pool with a slide and a well-maintained vegetable garden area when I tour behind the privacy fence.

A perfectly manicured Bermuda grass lawn, expertly trimmed boxwoods, and a pair of impressive oak trees in the front yard belie any recent marital issues. If I were shown a picture of this home with no other information, I would believe it's where one of the elusive well-functioning nuclear families in America resides.

My girl did good. I'm proud that Gemma was able to bring her dream to life.

It makes my chest hurt that it became her nightmare today.

"April." Chase gestures for me from the porch. The officer standing next to him studies me as I walk the pathway.

"April, this is Officer Buzz Slater. He is the one who made it possible for us to see your friend's house."

Buzz extends his hand to me. "I'm sorry about your friend," he says.

I accept his warm, calloused hand and feel the strength of his core energy. It reminds me of copper. Strong, pure, and bright, yet malleable enough to bend when necessary.

"Thank you," I whisper.

He nods and inhales deeply through his nose. "So we are clear before we begin,"—Buzz scans the three of us, making eye contact with each—"this is strictly off the books. If anybody ever asks, it didn't happen."

I'm taken aback by his statement but nod my agreement, as do my brothers.

"If the chief of police found out that I allowed this, they would probably put me up for psychological evaluation. Still, one of my aunts used to have premonitions. She saved my life one night by calling me and asking if I was wearing my vest. I wasn't. I don't like the extra bulk. But she is my aunt—, so I promised to put the vest on to get her off the phone. Forty-five minutes later, while answering a domestic dispute call, I went to put handcuffs on the husband to take him in to let him cool off, and his wife shot me in the chest."

"Dang," Chase says.

Buzz favors Chase with a wry grin. "Right. I didn't see that one coming. But the reason why I'm telling you this is I don't understand psychic readings, and I'm not superstitious. Still, I can't deny that folks like yourself might have some abilities. Abilities that might allow us to find a little boy tonight. And if there is a five percent chance that you can offer some help, I'm not going to be the one to prevent you from helping because your methods are unconventional."

The expectations of the three men weigh heavily on me. It only adds to the pressure I am putting on myself to find Jaxx and extricate him from danger. As if it will absolve me for being such a crummy friend.

"I hope I can help." My voice cracks.

"One other thing, I have to warn you that it's not pretty inside the house. We haven't called in the cleaning crew yet because we want to wait until forensics finishes their initial review and confirm they don't need a second pass. The entire scene has already been photographed and tagged, but as much as possible, if you can refrain from touching too many things, it would be helpful," Buzz says.

I think to explain that my best reads often come from touching items, but I decide to cross that bridge when we get there. There is a high likelihood that I won't even feel a spark of energy. If that is the result, touching personal items won't help. If what minor psychic abilities I have left decide to come to the forefront, I'll use them, but I can't force them if they don't flow.

Buzz gestures for us to follow him in, and my brothers step aside for me to go first.

Gemma's home has a formal living room to the right of the foyer. Immaculately decorated with hunter-green walls, a floral pattern loveseat, and high back chairs in either corner, the space belongs in an issue of *Southern Living*. The oak coffee table in the center of the room is void of everything except a stack of colorful coasters. A dining room with an extended cherry table seating eight and a China cabinet displaying three rows of decorative plates is to our left.

"Officer Slater, what did Gemma do for a living?"

The outer edges of his eyes crinkle, but he doesn't ask the obvious question of why I don't know when I'm her friend. "Gemma and her sister are both nurses. Tracy, her sister, works third shift at the hospital, so the two of them can always have someone available for Jaxx."

I struggle to tamp down my emotions again. It's conflicting to feel so happy for Gemma's success while being crushed by her death. Of course, she was a nurse. She was excellent with the sciences. I can envision her as one of the nurses who can handle the most demanding situations, like an emergency room nurse.

I remember extraordinarily little about Tracy, her sister. But I would be surprised if Gemma didn't strongly influence her to finish her nursing degree.

They appear to have built a wonderful life. Two economically disadvantaged young girls pull themselves up by the bootstraps and become successful citizens. It is a real feel-good story until somebody decides to ruin it.

The foyer opens into a large open floor plan. Stairs to the left lead to the second floor, and the wall in front of me is all windows with French doors in the middle.

I grin when the swimming pool with a slide comes into view. The backyard continues behind the pool house, and I believe I spy a garden area at the back right corner.

The bloodstains in the kitchen area cause me to swallow forcefully. Buzz strides toward the counter, and I follow him.

"Like I said, Tracy works the third shift. She arrived home at 7:45. The door was locked, and when she entered"—he gestures toward the foyer—"the blood was too obvious to miss. Gemma was already dead, and Jaxx was gone."

I step past Buzz into the kitchen and try to drop any of the mental partitions I built in my mind. Now that I'm here and see what was ruined, I want to feel what happened. I must feel Gemma's pain and see her attacker if I am to help.

"There was no forced entry, so we feel it was someone she knew," Buzz continues.

I close my eyes and focus all my power on the core of my body. I imagine pulling all the random energy in the room toward my sternum.

This was the method I used when I was younger to "read" a room, to scavenge the residual energies in a room and be able to read them.

At one time, my psychic abilities were strong and out of control. I heard voices night and day in my mind. The constant chatter nearly drove me insane.

Peculiar shadows would appear in my room, only to

materialize into disembodied faces or humanoid forms.

More commonly, if I touched someone who had criminal intent, a collage of their deviant visions would download into my mind. It often left me nauseous to the point of vomiting.

Nana Hirsch, my grandmother, whom the town accurately considers a witch, saved me from going crazy. She taught me how to build mental partitions that safely tucked my psychic abilities into the far corners of my mind.

I'm forever grateful to her for that instruction. The only thing is, I'm afraid it was like locking my skills up and throwing away the key. Today, just this once, I wish I still had the abilities.

This has the feel of an exercise in futility. I'm sure I won't be able to read anything. Still, if I do, I fear it may be a torrent of information flooding my mind as if a long-standing dam has burst.

Both scenarios make me apprehensive, and I pause with the collected energy impotent in my chest as I become fearful of failure as well as the possible success and what scars it may leave on my mind.

You must try, April.

Yes. I must. For Gemma. For Jaxx.

Cool perspiration forms on my scalp as I hold my concentration and the tail of the collected energy as long as I dare. I mentally force my mind open and hope I see my friend, that she sends me a vision, or at the very least I feel her presence in the room.

Nothing.

Even though I haven't tried this method of gleaning residual emotions from an area in years, I am mildly dismayed I felt nothing. Given the violence perpetrated in Gemma's home, I thought there would be something. Instead, not even a prickle on the back of my neck or hairs standing up on my arms. It's as if I have finally gotten my wish. I'm an ordinary woman with no "gifts."

Isn't that the story of my life? Abysmal timing.

I avoid the stares of the three men as long as I can. Biting my lower lip, I shake my head.

Dusty's eyes open wider. "Really?"

"I'm sorry."

"Man, I just knew with all the emotions that must have played out in this kitchen that you would pick something up," Dusty says.

I groan. "I know. Ten years ago, for sure. But I have been trying to tell you, Dusty. I make it a point not to use *any* of those abilities, and like anything, eventually, you lose the skill."

"Hey, I know I don't know how all this stuff works, but maybe it's not that your skills are gone. Maybe they're not warmed up yet. Nobody ever loses a skill. They might be rusty, but you still got the skill," Chase interjects.

I stare at Chase and try not to appear condescending. I think I fail, but he ignores my annoyance.

"I bet rather than having lost it, the problem is lack of familiarity. I bet because you haven't seen Gemma for so long, you can't pick up on her energy signature."

"It just doesn't work like..." Bless it. Why even bother trying to explain. I can tell by all three of their expressions I'm in this for the long haul.

"Sort of like a bloodhound," Buzz interjects.

"That is exactly what I'm thinking," Chase says. "She needs something of Gemma's to pick up on her energy. Then from there, maybe she can decipher who her attacker was."

My jaw drops open as I listen to their stupidity. It's incredible how people who don't have psychic abilities think it's all nice, neat, and predictable. I look at Dusty and rotate my hands, palms up, gesturing for him to help me.

Dusty should understand, given he has a touch of the "gifts." Rather than offering to end the novices' prescription for improving April's ability, he simply shrugs his shoulders.

Thanks for the assist, big guy.

"Gemma's bedroom is upstairs. It's already been examined, and I suppose we could let April touch a few of Gemma's personal items." Buzz turns his attention to me. "Would that help?"

At least he has the good sense to ask. "I don't really think so."

Buzz stops in his tracks, considering my negative response.

"Still, if there's even the slightest chance it helps, we're talking about a five-year-old boy, April," Chase says.

Pigs will fly before I go fishing with Chase. Bassmaster tournament be darned. He shouldn't be pressing me like this.

Still, there is no predicting what will kick my paranormal abilities into action. I suppose I'd prefer to have tried and failed than hear about something dreadful happening to Jaxx a month from now and wonder if Buzz and Chase's request might have made a difference.

"I didn't say we couldn't try. I said I doubt it will work," I say to save face.

There are two bedrooms at the top of the stairs. To the left, I see a little boy's bed made out to look like a NASCAR stock car with a big head sticker of Derek Thomas in a Crimson Tide uniform running the ball on the wall. In between the two rooms is a bathroom. The bedroom to the right is painted in lilac and fuchsia. The colors clash something awful, and I grin, remembering they are Gemma's two favorite colors. True to form, she will not give much credence to people's opinions of what colors match and don't match in her space.

Standing in her room, I take in the canopied queen-size bed with lace comforter and the highly polished furniture. Everything in this room, and what I can see of the en suite bathroom from where I stand, is in perfect condition.

How did she manage this with a full-time job and a kid to raise? I have difficulty getting my clean clothes folded and into my dresser and remembering to take out the garbage on Wednesday morning.

The men take turns picking up different items and handing them to me. A glass unicorn figurine with a purple horn, the TV controllers, her toothbrush, and eight other things.

I was wrong in one sense. After not feeling anything in the kitchen, I was positive there was no place in the home with residual emotions. But I feel something now. I feel profoundly sad that I didn't keep in touch with this extraordinary woman. Even amid this tragedy and her death, I can't help but be so proud of her and wish I had been able to share in her accomplishments.

Once again, I convict myself as the worst friend ever.

We spent countless hours practicing and hundreds more watching silly movies. Gemma would beg me to hang out and watch her favorite real-crime stories. All those hours of fellowship were not enough to compel me to stay in touch with her.

The thought gives me pause, and I freeze as I turn it over in my mind.

"Officer Slater."

"Please, call me Buzz."

"Is Gemma's car still here, or did y'all take it in for the forensic team to go through it?"

He squints his eyes. "They checked it out while they were here. There is no reason to think it had anything to do with the crime."

"But it's here?" I ask again.

He gestures out the bedroom door. "Yes. The garage is off the kitchen."

I exit Gemma's bedroom and take the stairs two at a time. I don't wait for the men to catch up.

Entering the kitchen, I open my mind again. It doesn't hurt to try a second time.

No surprises, still nothing. Not even a tickle of energy.

As I walk through the mudroom and open the door to the garage, I'm even more confident that I'm right. If nothing else, Gemma was reliable in doing what she said she would do.

I open the door of the red "soccer mom" SUV. The sight of the child's car seat in the back pulls hard at my heart. I take a second to draw a steadying breath.

Leaning over, I run my hand under the driver's seat. I begin to doubt myself. My finger pushes up against an envelope, and I feel the tape holding it to the underside of the seat.

Taking my time, I peel each corner slowly before pulling the paper free from the seat's base. My heart beats wildly as I open the envelope.

I hear the men tromping through the mudroom.

"What do you have there?" Buzz asks.

I hold the piece of paper toward them. "I know who killed Gemma."

 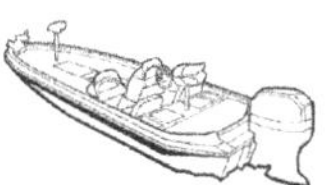 

Chapter 6

Officer Slater finishes reading the letter from Gemma. He exhales out his mouth. "Stephen has an alibi. Not even an hour after Tracy found Gemma, we interviewed him at his home. We also know that Gemma was still alive at seven o'clock because Tracy called her to tell her she was on her way home."

"Buzz, she is telling you—" "—I point at the letter in his hand —"right there that Stephen wants her dead."

He nods but fails to look me in the eye. Folding the letter carefully by its creases, he slides it back into the envelope. "I understand. And in cases like this, an ex-husband is a prime suspect. Until we've established an alibi.

"Still, the timing doesn't work for what we have already established. Gemma was killed between seven and seven forty. We were at Stephen's door by eight." Buzz rubs his hand over his stubbled chin. "Besides, somebody took Jaxx, and he wasn't at Stephen's."

He looks me in the eye and arches his brow. The silence hangs between us as we stare at one another.

I break first. "Well, I'm afraid that is all I have to offer."

Buzz clasps his hands together at his chest. "Thank you. I appreciate you trying. I knew it was a long shot, but I will try any method if it might give us a clue where to look for Jaxx."

"What now? Where are y'all going to canvas search for him?"

Buzz favors me with a tight smile as he shrugs. "Exactly. The community is ready to mobilize a search party for him. But I don't know where to ask them to search. We know he is not with any family members, which is unfortunate. This looks more like a random crime, which is the bane of any investigator's life."

None of us speak on the short drive home. The trip results are what I anticipated from the beginning. However, for one flittering moment, when I felt the edge of the envelope Gemma left, I dared to hope something positive might come from our attempt.

My brothers appear entirely dejected.

"What time did you change your flight to?" Chase asks Dusty as we turn into our parents' neighborhood.

"It's a six a.m. red-eye. I should make the meeting in Miami with fifteen minutes to spare."

"Do you need a ride?"

"Thanks, but I'm just gonna park in the long-term lot. It's only until Sunday."

I'd like to know more about what is going on with Dusty and the situation with his ex-wife, Bethany. Right now, I'm too mentally exhausted to ask.

"Since you're here until in the morning, what do you say to us cooking some weenies in the fire pit?" Chase asks.

"Sure, that'll work," Dusty says.

"Sure," I croak. My throat is still too tight from fighting back all the frustrated emotions balled up inside me.

Chase pulls into my parents' driveway. We exit and approach our home in a manner that reminds me of walking toward the chapel doors for the funeral of a friend. Our silence offers no distraction from my failure.

Dusty peels off to the right, taking the path toward the fire pit close to the shoreline. Daddy built it when we first moved in. It's positioned twenty yards up from the foxtails that populate the shallows on the left-hand side of our property. The walkway to the dock is to the right of the rectangular-shaped gray stone pit.

The structure is much larger than is necessary these days. My brothers will build a five-log fire typically.

When we were younger, the pit was too small. Back then, we built mammoth bonfires that often threatened to catch neighboring boathouses on fire. Orange embers would take flight on the hot air currents only to float down as tiny firebombs on top of surrounding houseboats. Fortunately for us, nothing ever caught fire back then, and they are more cautious now.

I follow Chase into the kitchen. "Do you need a hand?"

He favors me with a wan smile. I know he is trying hard to conceal his disappointment, but it's not coming easy for him.

Chase has a huge soft spot for children. I always imagined he would be the dad in a real-life version of *Cheaper by the Dozen*. Only much kinder and a lot more fun.

Yet here he is in his early thirties, and he still hasn't found his leading lady for that story.

"Mom got some hot dog buns yesterday." He points toward the cupboard.

I find the buns and a pack of marshmallows behind them. "Do you want these marshmallows?"

He looks over his shoulder as he pulls a pack of hot dogs and the condiments from the fridge, setting them on a metal tray. "Sure. I don't think we have the rest of the ingredients to make smores."

"That's okay. Toasted marshmallows would be nice now. Sort of like comfort food to soothe this hurt inside." I notice him staring at me with a pained expression. "What?"

"I don't get it, April. When you lived here, you said you felt and heard things all the time."

The question doesn't bother me. I can understand why Chase is confused. "I did. Yet now, it's rare. An occasional déjà vu moment or a dream that might portend the future. But I can never be certain."

I consider telling him that a similar dream convinced me to come to Guntersville this weekend. Still, I don't want to muddle my explanation. "But the whole feeling energies and seeing ghosts..." I shrug. "It's so unusual now, I might as well say it doesn't exist for me any longer."

"But how?"

"Not using that freaky skill set—and I think not being here played a big part in it, too." I look out the glass wall of the kitchen and see Dusty lighting the fire. "There is a lot of random energy in Guntersville. When I'm here, I feel the skills vibrating inside of me. But they don't pop into use like they used to without me trying to bring them forward."

Chase picks up the tray. "So you learned to control them, but what good is that if you killed them off?"

"Loads." I laugh. "My goal is to be normal, Chase. I don't want to be a version of Granny or, heaven forbid, Nana."

His brow furrows before he turns from me. "You could do worse, you know." He slides the glass door open too roughly, and it bangs on its frame.

I regret my careless comment. I forget how much the boys worship our grandmothers. Still, if I must choose between a Baptist zealot and an animus witch, I choose to leave town.

Each of my grandmothers is a *special* classification of odd in their own way. Granny Snow may look like a sweet little church lady, but she believes her prayers can materialize things she desires out of thin air. She also believes that both demons and angels walk the earth. If she didn't have the Bible to back up her beliefs, I think she would be as much of a social outcast as my Nana.

Nana has a commanding, forceful persona. Which explains where Mama got her personality.

Since Nana's religion hasn't been socially acceptable since the Vikings were converted to Christianity, she lives out in the woods in seclusion. I think both she and the citizens of Guntersville prefer the arrangement.

I close the sliding door behind me and follow Chase down to

the fire pit.

The boys can't understand because they don't have my "gifts." Every time I see one of my grandmothers, I worry that I'm a freakish combination of the two women. An anomaly that should not exist.

From the boys' standpoint, I'm sure both grandmothers are a real hoot. I'm convinced that is why they make it a point to check in on the grandmothers regularly. But neither Dusty nor Chase need worry that they are looking at a version of themself forty years in the future. Perspective is paramount.

The kindling around the logs Dusty formed in a teepee-shaped formation catches fire. Chase sets the tray of weenies down on the edge of the fire pit.

Dusty lifts two of the weenie forks off the hook on the side of the pit. "Choose your weapon," Dusty says as he holds them out toward Chase.

Chase selects his fork and flips it into the air, catching it by its wooden handle. "En garde!" He lifts his left hand in the air and points the weenie fork at Dusty with his right.

Dusty laughs as he raises his fork and swipes at Chase. The two fire pit utensils make contact, creating a dull thud.

Making sure to avoid their mortal combat—I'm not fond of the emergency room—I set the buns and marshmallows on one of the stumps that we use as seats around the pit.

I've seen this feature show of Jack Sparrow dueling Captain Hook at least a hundred times in my life, and I know how it ends. Always with someone getting hurt, and it’s usually Dusty because Chase is the better athlete with exceptional reflexes.

“Y’all, stop before somebody gets hurt."

"Your sister is afraid I'm going to hurt you." Dusty laughs.

"She's just afraid she will have to fight the winner," Chase says.

Dusty makes an awkward lunge toward Chase. Chase doesn't anticipate it, and the rod of his weenie fork slaps Dusty on the wrist.

Dropping his fork, Dusty grabs his wrist. "Dagnabbit, that smarts."

"Dude, what were you doing?"

"Trying to stab you."

Chase laughs uncontrollably and takes a seat on one of the stumps. "Seriously, I don't mean to laugh. Are you okay?"

"Yeah, I guess. I better go get some ice to put on it. Bethany will be furious tomorrow if I can't sign that huge check for her." Dusty lumbers back up the path toward the back porch.

"Hey, make yourself useful and bring some beer down on that return trip, good buddy," Chase says.

"What the heck. Do I look like your butler or something?" Dusty raises his right hand. "And I'm on injured reserve."

"Ah, don't be that way. I'll warm your weenie up for you if you get the beer," Chase says and flashes a grin.

Dusty laughs as he steps onto the porch. "Forget the beer. As bad as my wrist hurts, I'm breaking out the Jack."

"That'll work too."

Chase turns his attention to the hot dogs. I watch as he puts two on three different forks.

"The part of the Shadow today will be played by April May," Chase says in his best announcer's voice as he hands me one of the forks. "You're awfully distant. Are you thinking about Gemma?"

I shake my head. "No. I'm actually thinking about her little boy."

Chase holds the other two forks above the flames. "Does that help? Can you have a delayed read or something that will tell Buzz where to search?"

"They have a lead. Gemma told them who to look at," I grumble.

Chase nods as he turns the forks over. "Maybe."

"Maybe? So, you believe like the police that Stephen is innocent?"

Chase locks eyes with me and squints. "Lord, no. I think he is as guilty as the day is long. For one thing, it's too much of a coincidence that a man who has a custody dispute with his ex, suddenly finds himself the only parent of his child. That would be extremely fortunate for Stephen, and I don't believe for a moment he is that lucky."

"Then why doesn't Buzz charge him?"

"There is an enormous difference between logical assumptions and facts, April. The only fact Buzz has to go on at the moment is that Stephen has an alibi. Of course, that doesn't mean that he didn't hire someone else to kill Gemma. Or who knows, maybe hired someone to kidnap his son, and when Gemma tried to stop him, he got violent and accidentally killed her."

This whole situation stinks to high heaven. What Chase says makes sense. There is a good chance Gemma wasn't supposed to be hurt.

His logic only serves to frustrate me as I realize we may never know her killer's intent. Since the result is Gemma is dead, the intent is irrelevant. I change the subject.

"What is the story with Dusty and Bethany?"

Chase becomes highly interested in the hot dogs he is roasting.

"*Chase*," I sing. "Come on. Share."

"Lord, April. You know I don't get involved in that stuff."

"Do you expect me to believe that?"

He cuts his eyes toward me. "All I know is when Bethany catches wind he has another book release, she asks the court to up her alimony."

"Why?"

Chase chuckles. "Uh-uh. That is all I got to say about that. If you want to learn more, you need to ask him yourself."

Fair. I wouldn't want Chase telling Dusty anything without my knowledge.

"Have you been seeing anybody?" I ask.

His eyebrows raise as he nods. "I actually have."

A flash of excitement makes me lean forward. It's been ten years since Chase dated anyone. "Who?"

"Well," Chase drawls. "Today, I saw you and Dusty and Buzz —"—"

I make a rude noise and lean back on my stump. "You're so funny."

He gestures toward me with one of his forks. "You know your weenies are not gonna roast themselves."

As my brothers and I eat hot dogs, drink Jack and Coke, and roast marshmallows, it occurs to me that our relationship has changed over the years. The twins have an inseparable bond despite being complete opposites as they are in looks and thoughts. They were and always have been yin and yang, neither whole without the other.

Me, their kid sister, they always made sure to include when and wherever they can. I know unequivocally that is the reason I find it easy to relate to my male friends. Yes, I was Mama's satellite, but I was always part of my brothers' group.

For the first time in my life, I feel like a third wheel. They're not doing it intentionally. So many of the things they discuss happened while I was at college. Understandably, they don't bother to go into much detail and bring me up to speed because they know I'm about to move away and start my life somewhere else.

That is my decision. And although I am excited about my move to Atlanta this summer, my feelings are becoming sore because I'm no longer in their unique group.

That is okay. Soon, I'll have a fantastic condo in downtown Atlanta and hundreds of new friends to sit around and talk to during one of my many parties.

Dusty stands and stretches. "I better hit the sack." He looks at his phone. "I've got time for a three-hour nap."

"You want me to set my alarm, too? Just to make sure you get up?" Chase asks.

"Nah. No need to do that. I sit my phone on the other side of the bedroom. Once my feet hit the floor, I'll be wide awake."

"All right. Well, safe flight, and don't do anything that will get you fifty years to life."

Dusty rolls his eyes. "She ain't worth that."

"I'm not gonna agree with you in case you two remarry in a few years."

"Yeah, right. If that happens, I expect you to do the honorable thing a loving brother would do and shoot me in the head." Dusty walks over to me and awkwardly gives me a one-arm hug, kissing me on the forehead. "That is a bad break today. I'm sorry. But you keep your eye on the ball and become the success we know you will be. I think your friend Gemma would have wanted that for you."

"Thanks."

He stares at me, smiles, then turns toward the house.

Chase and I return to our companionable silence as we watch the fire.

I've obviously drank too much Jack Daniels. My stomach is queasy, and as I stare at the dying embers, I feel like I'm rotating around the fire pit.

"You about ready to go in, Tink?"

The childhood nickname harkens back to a simpler time. I can't help but wonder why Chase would call me that now when he hasn't in years. "You go ahead. I think I'll stay out here for a few more minutes. The silence is helping me get my thoughts together."

"I hate to leave you out here by yourself. I can stay a little longer if you like."

"No, I'm good. Thanks."

Chase pokes at the fire with a long stick. The last log rolls over, burying most of the embers in ash. In my periphery, he stands and appears ready to say something. He shrugs and takes the path back to the house.

While I stare at the diminishing embers, I have the perfect pity party. I don't understand how I'm supposed to manage everything in my life and get what I want. It seems that anytime I progress with my personal goals, I'm doing so at the expense of my relationships. I also know from experience that relationships take time, lots of time, to keep them healthy. Time I need to make my goals a reality.

How do I do both? I want to do both. I really do. Yet I am stuck in this constant conflict of competing interests, and when it's all said and done, I'm just left sad. Sad for the relationship with Gemma that could have blossomed into a beautiful adult friendship that will never be. Still, if I take too much care with my friends and family, I will not be the high-profile defense attorney I know I am destined to be.

My head is spinning even worse now. Nausea continues to build in my stomach. Still, I have half a Solo cup full of Jack and Coke, and never let it be said that April May Snow doesn't finish the job.

I raise my cup for another sip, and the noise behind me makes me come off my stump. I swivel, and a massive shadow on the porch comes into view.

"Come on in, April. You had a rough day. You need to get some sleep."

Dusty is channeling a mama bear. I start giggling as I think of him as a bear. If he were a bear changeling, it wouldn't take much for him to transform. Given his thick build and the fact that he is the furriest person I know, he is halfway there.

"Are you coming?"

I wave him off. "I will in a few. I'm gonna watch the last of these flames in the pit die down." Looking to the pit, I realize there is no longer a glow from the fire.

He doesn't answer. I hear the glass door open again. "As you wish. Stay away from the water."

"Will do." I wave my hand over my head.

The glass door shuts, and I return to the brooding I have mastered.

If I were smart, I would quit drinking. It's as if I am attempting to punish myself by becoming sick.

I stare at the dead fire and swear it is wavering like a mirage. Truthfully, I'm not sure if it's the black, charcoaled wood chunks wavering or my vision. Either way, the movement makes my gorge rise. The ketchup from the hot dogs I ate takes on a metallic taste.

A fish splashes in the water to my left. The catfish under the dock my brothers feed have become huge in their advanced age. One must have found a fat beetle or a juicy tadpole to snack on.

I wonder if there is any way I can help the police find Jaxx. Without paranormal skills. I'm smart. Maybe if I think on it long enough, I can come up with some...

There is another slapping sound in the water. I squint into the darkness.

Like I could see a catfish from where I sit. Unless it jumped a foot out of the water.

Grabbing a marshmallow from the still-open bag, I toss it toward the lake. "Have a snack, then it's lights out for you, young man."

I focus back on the fire as I grab a stick and poke it. A handful of glowing orange chunks are exposed, giving a slight illumination around the pit.

The stupid fish causes another slapping sound to my left. I squint into the darkness.

That catfish must be eighty pounds to make so much racket.

I stand and throw the remaining ice cubes from my drink onto the embers. Above the hiss of the cubes being turned to steam, I hear water falling.

That is an odd sound to be hearing. My chest tightens as I swivel to look out at the lake while taking a step backward.

I still don't see anything. The sensation of spiders crawling up my spine tells me that it's not just my overindulgence in Jack Daniels causing the queasiness in my stomach. Focusing on the silhouette of the foxtails in the lake's shallows, I continue walking backward up the inclined path toward the back porch.

The sound of water falling into the lake continues.

A pinpoint of violet light pierces the night. It sways side to side, inches above the swollen foxtail heads.

My progress toward the house stops as my feet freeze in place.

The colorful light grows and brightens as I attempt to discern what it could be. My focus is on the glow, which looks like a tiny star suspended three feet above the lake's surface.

The focal point of my vision is too narrow. I gasp as I make out the humanoid silhouette emerging from the lake.

What the devil?

My eyes open so wide with fear, I worry my eyeballs will pop out any second. Yet, my feet won't listen to my brain and get a move on to the back porch.

My brain aches even more, and I realize I've stopped breathing.

As my eyes adjust to the darkness, I can make out the form of the entity. The glowing purple light appears to be centered on its chest.

I need to run, but my fight-or-flight reflexes are frozen.

With only ten yards between us, the shadow human lifts a hand toward me, and its fingers extend in my direction.

Oh, heck no!

My feet and legs finally listen to the excellent advice from my brain, and I don't even bother to backtrack now. I chug up the incline so fast that I'm out of breath as I hit the glass door.

I pull on the handle with everything I've got, and as the tendons in my fingers strain, two fingernails break, and the door doesn't budge. Peaches! Somebody locked the door.

Balling both my hands into fists, I pound on the glass. "Open up!"

Looking over my shoulder, I pray that this is something my drunk mind and overactive imagination have created. Instead, I watch the shadow person near the base of the porch. It's as if a giant-sized hand grabs my lungs and crushes them.

The glass shakes in its frame as I continue to beat on the door with both fists, screaming with my cheek pressed to the smooth, flat surface as I watch the shadow move closer. I pray one of my brothers is still up and can hear me.

There is no mistaking the feeling. Tingly power races from the back of my knees up to my neck. I'm too close to this paranormal event, and it's waking up my supernatural gifts. I'm running out of time.

Chapter 7

The kitchen light comes on. Dusty, his body hair giving him the appearance of wearing a bodysuit made of red, furry wool with a pair of Superman boxers pulled over the suit, stands at the landing of the stairs squinting toward the door.

"Dusty!" I'm hitting the door so hard now I may not need him to open it. I might break through it. "Open the stupid door!"

He comes to life and jogs to the door. Flipping the latch, he pulls it open.

I slide past him, leaving him in the doorway. The cold tingle ceases immediately.

"I am so sorry," Dusty says as he pulls the door shut and locks it. "I guess it's just a force of habit to lock the door."

I step to the side, looking past my brother to the porch. The purple light is gone. Somehow I knew it would be.

"What's gotten into you anyway?" he asks. "You look like you've seen a ghost."

I cut my eyes to him. His comment leaves me wondering if his peon paranormal skills caught the energy disruption. If so, he should be clued in that we dove into the deep end of the otherworldly scary pool. More likely, it is simply an unfortunate coincidence that he used that cliché at the most inappropriate moment.

I think he felt it. His voice sounds on edge, and it's more than the embarrassment of locking his sister out in the dark.

"I really am sorry," he pleads.

I shake my head. "It was an accident. Forget about it."

He sighs. "It's only that you already had an awful day. I sure didn't plan to make it worse by locking you out."

Still no freaky lavender light and no bipedal shadow. Even though the light from the kitchen is causing a minor glare on the glass door, I'm confident that the entity has dissipated.

I turn my attention back to my brother. "You've got to get up in a few hours, and if I'm honest about it, I'm beat."

"Are you sure you're all right?"

I force a smile, hoping that it will put him at ease. "I'm fine. Even if you had not heard me to let me in, I could have slept on one of the lawn chair loungers. It's not that big of a deal."

He isn't buying the last statement. I may have laid it on a little thick. Instead of arguing, though, he nods.

"All right. I'm going back to bed as long as you swear you are okay."

"Go. I'm fine."

He takes a step toward the stairs and turns back. "I guess the next time I'll see you is your graduation."

I grin at my furry brother. "I'm asking all the family to refer to it as 'Independence Day.'"

Dusty raises his eyebrows as he chuckles. "It's your special day. If that is what you want me to call it, consider it done."

I watch him walk to the landing at the top of the staircase and pivot to go down to the basement.

When he disappears, I turn and look out the glass door. Good. Still nothing.

My bedroom feels a little more foreign to me every time I spend the night in Guntersville. I close the door and do something I never do—lock it.

I know. Logically it makes no sense. If the shadow can walk

through the foxtails without making them tremble, it's doubtful a lock on a hollow-core bedroom door will pose any sort of obstruction.

One of the wonderful things about still having a room at my parents' home is that I don't have all my clothes in Tuscaloosa. I strip down to my panties and pull on an oversized beefy T-shirt to sleep in.

Today goes down as the suckiest day in history. It will be a struggle to even act like I want to go fishing with Chase. I have too much on my mind with Gemma's death, and now something with a glowing purple heart appearing out of the shallows trying to touch me with its freaky, long shadow fingers, to humor my brother.

Still, on the positive, it isn't the old man of the lake. I'm sure of it. I initially froze in fear because I have always been terrified that he would rise from the water and take me with him one day.

When I was a kid, the male ghost inhabiting the lake near my parents' boathouse once grabbed my ankle and pulled me underwater. After that event, I heard a recurrent voice and saw shadows occasionally form into something more solid. Okay, ghosts.

I refer to him as the old man because he sounds older when he speaks to me—in my head. That is not all. He also sounds like a psychopath who is obsessed with me.

But the shadow tonight was feminine. That distinction wasn't something I could see. I felt it.

Because I'm tired, I turn the light out. Still, I hold my phone and flip through social media as I wonder if there is any chance I might pass out due to exhaustion. That would be mercifully welcomed at this stage.

Rain strikes the roof and builds in intensity quickly. The rain beats down so fiercely, making a roaring sound on top of the roof. It's a regular toad strangler.

My initial alarm quells. I lived through the Guntersville tornado of 2011. God didn't take me then, and if he wants me tonight, there won't be much I can do about it.

I'm a Southern girl. I don't shrink in the presence of tornados and hurricanes.

Still, I check the weather radar. Peaches! This is going to be an all-night affair.

I consider going to sleep in Dusty's room in the basement. No. The stairs are just through the kitchen. I can be in his room in less than a minute if I need to be. It's not like a tornado can sneak up on me tonight—since I doubt I'll sleep a wink.

The roar outside my window takes up less of my attention. My eyes are heavy as I read the same sentence several times on the newsfeed I'm scanning on my phone. Distant thunder rumbles, and the boom echoes toward our house.

Once I convinced myself the entity coming out of the water earlier was female rather than the old man, a part of me hoped it was Gemma. I'm proud that I've been able to extinguish my weird "gifts" before moving to Atlanta and starting my new career. Still, I wouldn't mind being a tool for Gemma to help Jaxx from her grave. I would gladly backslide a little in my endeavor if it meant I could help.

Bless it. I hadn't even thought about that until now, but I've already backslid.

That is the first entity I've seen in four months. Even when I came home for Christmas, I only heard the old man talk once, and that was when I left my jacket on the boat and had gone back down to the boathouse by myself.

In Atlanta, I can finish the transformation to normal once and for all. One thing is sure: if I were to stay in Guntersville, I would never get rid of this curse.

Lightning lights my room, and rumbling thunder vibrates my bed.

I pull in a long, deep breath and let it out slowly. I've got to get some sleep. If I could only push everything that happened today out of my mind for half a second, I would pass out.

The lightning illuminates my room with great white light. She stands at the side of my bed, staring at me.

My breath catches, and I roll to my right. As my feet strike the cold wooden floor, I reach for my lamp, knocking it to the floor.

I follow it down on my knees, touching every part but the switch. I find it and push it on. The light temporarily blinds me.

She is gone.

Rising from my crouched-over position on the floor, I peer cautiously over my bed. Nope, no weird stalker ghost.

Watching me sleep? That just gives me the heebie-jeebies.

I'm still not entirely convinced. I return my lamp to its place on the nightstand and rise. Slowly I circle my bed.

Still no sign of her.

My eyes go to the last place to check, and fear bubbles up inside me.

Yeah, no. I really don't care to check under my bed. If she is hiding under there—well, if she is hiding under there, I will have to go sleep in Dusty's room.

"Bless it, I hate this town."

I move to the foot of my bed and grab hold of the comforter. I want to be on my feet, because it's faster to get away if she is under the bed. So, I crouch over, supporting myself on one hand, and pull back the comforter with the other.

My breath catches. There is nothing but dust bunnies under my bed.

I'm grateful nothing says 'boo.' Still, I'm wired like I drank three energy drinks back to back. The chances of going to sleep tonight are not in my favor.

I settle back into bed. There is nothing worth reading in the news, so I go to my word puzzle and try to solve it.

It isn't inside her like I thought earlier. The purple light. It is a necklace, an amulet around her neck. She had a transparent nature, but the amulet almost appeared solid.

Of course, I don't want to dwell on it, but I find it weird that I'm experiencing a new spirit at our house. It's not like all spirits are bound to a particular area or piece of property. Still, like when we are alive, we have a tendency to stay in the familiar.

Still, even though I had never seen her before, she looked vaguely familiar to me.

I finish a word puzzle and start a fresh one.

What a coincidence. The first four words of the puzzle are ghost, spirit, power, and missing. It's as if it is tailor-made for the present situation.

Like Mama always says, “Real life is stranger than fiction.”

My phone is not in my hand, and I'm thirsty for orange juice. I walk into the kitchen and pour myself a glass.

It is void of the usual strong, tangy flavor. Someone must have left the carton open. It loses some of its zest with the introduction of too much air.

I rinse my cup out in the sink and notice that I have my jeans and moccasins on. Since I can't sleep, I should go for a walk.

But what about the ghost lady? She has gone back to the lake. I’m not sure how I know that or why I am so confident about it.

I'm already on the back porch. Too late now, anyway.

There are Cheetos strewn across the deck. When did that happen? I’m surprised the squirrels haven’t already scarfed them up.

The ground is mushy, but it does not soak through my moccasins. The rain has ceased.

Walking through the forest, the land slopes hard to my left. The leaves under my feet slide, and I don’t have sure footing.

Dread creeps into my consciousness. I try to ignore that I no longer remember choosing to walk in the forest. Still, it terrifies me.

How can I be that focused on my thoughts? What are my thoughts?

The uneasiness and dread build in my gut as I realize I'm not familiar with this forest. These are not the woods at the end of our street that I used to hike.

This property is distinctly more sloped and fuller of a preponderance of hardwood trees. The leaves from last fall have decayed and are slick with rain. They cushion my step, and all is silent in the forest except my labored breathing.

Where the tarnation am I?

A light mist falls from the canopy above. Looking up, I see the sky is entirely concealed by army-green foliage and thick, brown-gray branches.

I consider stopping; I don't want to get lost. Still, something pulls me forward, and I find it irresistible.

This is a bad idea. It's as if there is a hole in my memory, and regardless of whatever invisible force is pulling at me, I know it would be wise to get help.

I reach for my phone in my back pocket. It's not there. *Are you kidding me?*

If the queasy uneasiness isn't powerful enough to stop me, realizing my tether to humanity is missing fixes my resolve to ignore the energy tugging at me. How stupid do I have to be to go traipsing around in an unfamiliar forest without the ability to communicate if I need assistance? What if I slip and break an ankle? Or worse, get bitten by a snake.

Hearing footsteps and heavy breathing behind me, I rotate quickly and take two faltering steps backward as I lose balance.

The mature whitetail doe eyes me suspiciously. We stare each other down. Looking between her twitching ears, I notice there is a trail behind the deer, and I'm blocking her forward progress on the path.

I never was much of a hunter. Firing rifles and shotguns is fun. Killing stuff, even stuff you like to eat, is a bit too barbaric for me. Besides, sitting in a tree stand while I fight off frostbite in my toes and fingers isn't exactly what I consider an enjoyable time.

But, I do remember some of the lessons. A handy bit of advice from Chase comes to mind. "When you're lost, a deer trail is better than no trail."

True, I've never had the need to test his theory, and don't think that it doesn't give me pause to be relying on the wisdom of Chase, but now, it seems like the best option I have.

The doe snorts at me impatiently, stomps her front left hoof, and cuts to the side of me. I look over my shoulder and watch her continue down the slope. For the first time through the heavy foliage, I see Guntersville Lake at the bottom of the hill.

For a second, I consider following her to the lake. Even if I'm on the far side, I can always walk the perimeter until I find one of the many homes along the waterline.

The prickly feeling of paranormal energy convinces me to follow the trail away from the lake. Heaven help me. I hope this isn't as stupid of a decision as it seems.

My lungs and thighs burn as I climb up the steep slope. The decaying vegetation continues to slide out from under me randomly as I hike.

The trail turns hard to the right at the mountain's peak and continues along the ridgeline. Despite being at the mountain's apex, the hardwood, forty to fifty feet overhead, continues to block out any semblance of sky or sun. Despite being outside, I have a claustrophobic feeling beginning to niggle in my mind.

Yes, this was a stupid decision. I should have gone down to the lake.

The tingly sensation sits like a yoke over my shoulders now, and the base of my scalp prickles fiercely. There is some bad juju up ahead. That much is for sure.

The mist has intensified to rain and drops freely from the foliage above. The temperature has fallen, and the dominant scent has changed from oak and cinnamon to wet earth.

It's not too late to turn around. The safer bet is to follow the perimeter of the lake.

A squat shadow lies ahead. My shoulders tense. I'm sure that whatever I've been feeling has emanated from the sizable silhouette in the distance.

I hate the fact that my curiosity is always on hyperdrive. One of these days, it will get me into trouble I can't get out of.

Well, in for a penny in for a pound. I grit my teeth and walk toward the dilapidated structure.

As I close in on it, I recognize it as a small house. More accurately, it *was* a house before the roof gave way, collapsing in, and the vines overtook the walls. It's been abandoned for quite some time. A young hickory tree grows out from the center of the house.

I slow my gait to examine the house further, watching the rain splash off the remaining decayed shingles of the house. Rain pelts the path in front of me.

I'm not wet. The rain is not striking me.

There is a snort to my left. I turn my attention in the direction of the noise.

The doe's eyes, sharp and attentive from the ground where she lays, meet mine. I recoil in horror. As I step backward, I slip and fall onto my butt. I crab crawl away through the wet leaves as I watch the white maggots covering the doe undulate and ripple across her decaying body.

I know I'm screaming as I try to gain my footing, but I can't hear myself.

"April!"

Chase stands over me. The lights are on in my bedroom.

He removes his hand from my shoulder. "Hey, you need to get up."

I'm still reeling from the dream. It's the same one I continued to have in Tuscaloosa, except the Cheetos were on the porch and I went much further than in the past versions. I had never seen the deer or the house in my previous dreams.

"We don't have much time," he says.

I shake my head. "What are you talking about, Chase?"

"Buzz got a lead on where Jaxx might be. They're putting together a search party."

Chapter 8

It's cold this morning. The skies are gray and threaten more rain. A typical March in Alabama. If you don't like the weather, hang around for a bit, and it'll change.

Chase and I haven't said much since we got into his truck. He has the heater blowing full blast, but I still can't seem to get warm. Something tells me it's not just the temperature causing me to break out in gooseflesh on my arms.

I can't take my focus off my feet. I didn't want to put the moccasins on, especially considering my dream last night. Still, my hiking boots are in Tuscaloosa, and these were the shoes best suited for walking through the woods that were left in my closet at my parents' house.

There are a million reasons I don't want to help with the search. Given the dream and the current déjà vu of my footwear, it's scaring the bejesus out of me.

With Gemma's son's life in danger, I must bury my fear.

I'm groggy and hungry. It's no mystery why. I didn't sleep well last night, and Chase didn't give me any time to grab breakfast.

"Can we swing into a drive-thru and get a biscuit and a Dr. Pepper?"

Chase turns his attention to me. He has his hero face on. I know I'm out of luck before he answers me.

"Buzz said they would have biscuits and coffee there for the volunteers," Chase says.

I like coffee, but I could use the sugary rush of a Dr. Pepper to keep my eyelids open. But it's best not to try Captain America's patience. I'll suck it up and find some other way to get my sugar fix.

I would prefer to purge it from my mind. The image of the doe lying on her side and staring at me while maggots teem on the open wound that was her rib cage. Still, it is foremost on my mind, not necessarily for the grotesqueness of the image as the weirdness of her eyes still being alert. There must be some message hidden in that peculiarity, but I'll be darned if I can discern the vision.

The randomness of my "gifts" is one of the reasons why I absolutely detest them. If I could control them and if they were always predictable, I might find them helpful. But even though I've had this dream several times, I can't be sure that any aspect of it is valuable. It could be a nonsensical coincidental dream. Or, as my experiences have been in the past, it could foretell an event of great consequence.

Finding a dead deer next to an abandoned house doesn't seem to be something worthy of a paranormal event. I may have a deer stuck in my mind for some incidental reason. I mean, I think deer are pretty. Still, that line of logic to explain why I have a deer on my mind does not feel authentic.

Trying to figure out these gifts is going to drive me crazy.

One thing is sure. I'm making the right decision by not coming home after graduation. Especially now that there is one more apparition near my parents' house that is obsessed with me. Although I did not feel anything malicious from the ghost lady last night compared to the old man, I don't care. I'm done with being a magnet to things that shouldn't be anymore. I don't want to wake up and see dead things standing at the side of my bed.

I consider that a reasonable expectation for anyone.

The jostling of Chase's truck as he leaves the paved road brings me back to the present. He has turned onto a narrow logging road.

"How did they get this lead?" I ask Chase.

His lips narrow into a thin line, and he doesn't take his attention from the winding trail. "One of the other officers was staking out Stephen's house. Around one a.m., Stephen left, during the middle of that storm, and drove up here. The officer was suspicious that Jaxx was put away somewhere nearby. After backup arrived, they made their way up the trail. When they found Stephen, there was a confrontation."

I frown. "What do you mean a confrontation?"

Chase exhales loudly through his nose. "Stephen pulled a gun and fired at the police."

"Please tell me they were able to take him into custody."

"No. They were forced to return fire. Stephen was dead before he hit the ground."

I close my eyes and try not to think about the implication of this. If Stephen has Jaxx stored away somewhere, Jaxx's whereabouts may have died with his father.

As if he read my mind, Chase adds, "They're confident that Jaxx is nearby. It's a good break. We'll be able to find him and return him to his aunt."

That is one scenario. The optimistic one. I don't want to think about the other outcome, which seems more likely to me.

The trees give way to an open field. Thirty pickup trucks and a few gators are parked in the semblance of rows to our right. Buzz is standing in front of a group of seventy men and women, giving instructions to the horde.

I scarf down a cold sausage biscuit that sits in my stomach like a bowling ball. I try to get some caffeine in me via coffee. I don't know what brand of coffee Buzz brought to the search, and I've never tried chicory. Still, considering the odd wood-and-cherry taste lingering on my tongue after the first sip, I wonder if that's what it is. Blech.

My fear about the parallels between my dream and this morning subsides as Buzz explains how he wants us to work together in grids. That confirms that my dream was simply random. In the vision, I am always alone, besides the doe. With grids, someone should always be within view of me.

With this new knowledge, I feel more invigorated. I need to be. If there is any hope that we will find Jaxx, today will be our best chance.

The police are correct. It is challenging to believe Stephen drove to this remote site twenty miles outside of Boaz during a storm without an excellent reason. Like his son being stowed away near here.

But where? How do you hide a little boy in the woods and not risk him being hurt in the elements last night?

My stomach roils as I realize that is precisely why Stephen ventured out to this location last night. Surely he must have known the police would have him under surveillance. Yet he came out during the storm.

Because he knew Jaxx was in danger because of the weather.

The epiphany spikes my anxiety. I'm now more concerned about Jaxx's safety than ever.

Buzz assigns me to the far left of the seventy-five-person team. Chase is in the center with Buzz. Reese, a lady from Boaz I've never met, is a hundred feet away to my right.

The shrill of Buzz's whistle pierces the silence. Our line moves forward.

A few hundred yards into the search, I realize the futility of our task. This will be considerably more difficult than finding a needle in a haystack. We don't even know if we are headed in the right direction. Jaxx could be behind us.

The footing offered by the forest floor is not unlike that of my dream. With each step, I prepare for my foot to slide out from under me, and on several occasions, I surf a few feet down the slope and am forced to slow my pace. This all makes for a poor search. I'm sure I am as intent on keeping my balance as searching for suspicious landmarks that will indicate Jaxx's location.

With each slippery step, my expectations of finding the little boy today drop. Of course, I will finish the task at hand, working the grid that Buzz has requested us to search. Still, I am now positive that someone will have to step forward with new and specific information on his whereabouts if we are meant to find him. Someone who might have seen Stephen take his son through the woods.

It's not unheard of. No, it's not hunting season, so there won't be as many sportsmen in the woods as usual. Still, it's common for deer hunters to search out the next season's hunting areas during the spring.

That is an excellent thought, except that this is a weekday, and most hunters will be at work.

My feet slide out from under me, and I fall hard onto the wet leaves. I pop up like I am made of rubber and glare at my hands, now caked in pieces of rotting leaves. *Lovely.*

As much as I dread the fishing tournament, I now will gladly sit in Chase's bass boat and dutifully cast whatever color worm he declares the correct one for as long as he wishes. Anything would be better than this wild goose chase.

I hear a grunting noise to my right as if someone has been punched in the gut. I squint up the slope and make out some thick, short legs on the ground above me.

Reese doesn't move to get up, and I become concerned. "Reese, are you all right?" Reluctantly I turn to climb my way up the hill toward her.

"I think I'm too old for this," she grumbles.

The slope is particularly steep here, and where there are no wet leaves to make the footing treacherous, there is loose sandstone that crumbles when I step on it. I am relegated to grabbing hold of sapling branches and pulling myself up the hill. My hands are covered in sticky sap as I reach the oak tree that blocks most of Reese's body from my view.

"You didn't break anything, did you?" I ask.

She laughs. It has a hysterical note to it that makes me uneasy.

"Only my pride."

I hold my hand out to help her up.

She shakes her head. "No, deary. I'm going to sit here and rest for a spell."

I guess I understand. Reese isn't exactly built for speed or endurance. She was probably athletically challenged thirty years and sixty pounds ago, considering her shape.

"Will you be okay?"

"Sure." She waves her hand. "I'll be simply fine. You go on ahead, and I'll catch up."

She fidgets as I continue to stare at her. I'm concerned that she may have injured herself when she fell.

"Please. Finish the task. We've got to find that little boy."

I consider plopping down onto the leaves and keeping Reese company for the next few hours. Even though I don't know her and there is a significant age discrepancy between us, hanging out with a stranger must be better than continuing to struggle on the side of this mountain.

"Okay, I'll look for you on the way back."

She tries to smile, but I see the underlying concern in her eyes. "I'll be here."

Rather than go back to my position, I only walk halfway back down the slope. Being one search member down, I'll have to be extra vigilant and try to cover both lanes—Reese's and mine.

I can't help but consider that if Martin's girlfriend Penny hadn't so selfishly taken him away to her parents this weekend, I would be eating ribs at Dreamland about now. If uncle Norman hadn't decided to take Tricia up to Chicago, I'd be enjoying smoked chicken at Martin's barbecue. Dude, why have I got barbecue on my mind?

I pull my phone out of my pocket and am surprised to see it's already 11:30. Considering all I've had today is a cold sausage biscuit, it is a wonder I haven't fainted from low blood sugar.

The first of the rain strikes the foliage above, adding insult to injury. Awesome. I'm going to hit the trifecta on the misery scale: cold, wet, and hungry. I think I can safely throw thirsty onto my complaint pile within the hour, too.

Whose idea was it to go into the woods without backpacks? This missing-kid situation certainly has Chase discombobulated out of his usual "be prepared" Boy Scout ways.

I suppose once he got the call, he understood the urgency. The only thing is, I really believe the most critical item was to keep Stephen alive and take him into custody. I'm hoping against hope that it is not a failure of the police department that will cost Jaxx his life.

What I first thought to be a thick patch of kudzu comes into focus, and I see that it was once an 800-square-foot clapboard house. The only portion of it visible from this distance is the door left ajar, a broken aluminum window to the left of the door, and the gaping maw of a hole where the roof used to be. Now a cedar tree rises through it twenty feet.

I wipe the accumulating rain from my eyes and break to the right toward the dilapidated house. If Jaxx is alive—yes, I'm sorry to say I have begun to consider the alternate outcome—the derelict house is the best hiding place I have seen during my four-hour search.

It doesn't escape me that there are several similarities between what I see now and my recurring dream. Still, there are enough differences to satisfy me that they are unrelated.

Obviously, the tree in real life is a cedar, while it was a hickory tree in my dream. Not to mention I'm now as wet as if I had jumped in the lake, and in my dream, my clothes were dry.

There is little left of the three steps leading up to the front door. Two of the planks are completely gone and with the third, the dry rot is so pronounced I wouldn't dare attempt to step on it. I use the length of my legs to stretch and grab hold of the door frame to pull myself in through the open front door.

I wrinkle my nose in disgust and immediately wish I had not entered the structure. It's difficult to decide if I'm feeling something evil within the four walls or if it's simply the malodor.

Despite the desire to jump out of the old house, I force myself to examine the interior as carefully as possible. The kitchen is still intact, save for water damage. I carefully open each cupboard door. The hinges pull loose from one of the cabinets, and the door comes off in my hand. No young boy inside the cabinets.

There is one bedroom off to the back, but I now see that a large oak tree fell across that at one time and crushed the room. To my left, in the corner, is a preponderance of rat droppings and some tiny bones.

"Jaxx!" I yell.

The cabinets in the kitchen were the best opportunity to hide someone. There is no other place left intact enough to hide a young boy. Besides, if he were hidden here, he would surely respond when I yelled his name.

"Jaxx, we're here to take you home!"

I wait patiently and hope that I hear a young boy holler for help.

The rain increases its intensity, and rivulets stream down my face. My clothes are thoroughly soaked. If I had not found this dilapidated house, I would have already turned back to our rendezvous site.

"Jaxx! Don't be afraid. We're here to help."

Lightning cracks nearby, causing me to nearly jump out of my skin. The smell of ozone covers the stench of death in the house.

I'm dedicated, and I want to find Jaxx, but I don't care to get struck by lightning in some nasty old house out in the woods. I survey the corners one more time, give the kitchen another cursory review, and move toward the front door.

I jump down from the threshold. My feet slide when I land, but I steady myself with my left hand on the ground. As my line of sight rises, I see the doe fifty feet in front of me.

We stare at each other. Neither of us moves, and I hear my heart beating in my ears as raindrops crash down from the canopy above.

She snorts, turns, and lopes off at a leisurely pace. A small bundle remains where she stood.

Making my way over to the lump on the forest floor, I realize what it is and understand its significance. I snatch it off the ground and scream for the rest of the search team to rally to me.

 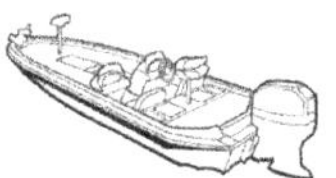 

Chapter 9

Chase's disappointment is unbearable.

Jaxx's aunt confirms to Buzz the stuffed Pooh Bear in the picture he sent her belongs to Jaxx. It is a substantial find by me. It precipitates the group spending an hour searching every inch of the old, dilapidated house.

Our spirits rose when Chase found a seam on the wood floor. Once we cleared away the leaf debris, we confirmed it was a trap door to a potato cellar. But we didn't find a young boy in the twelve-foot by fifteen-foot earthen room. Only a few wooden shelves remained, which had rotted with time and spilled the contents of their Mason jars rudely onto the dirt floor.

The cellar being empty is the worst kind of trick. It leaves us hollow and shattered after the brief, exciting possibility of finding Jaxx.

Chase's disappointment goes beyond the empty cellar and the missed day of the fishing tournament that could have been the doorway to a dream career. His disappointment is in me.

"Here, try again." He holds the wet and muddy bear out toward me again.

I roll my eyes and accept the stuffed toy from my brother. It's not that I don't want to be helpful. I just can't. "Chase, I'm sorry. I don't feel anything."

The lines at the edge of his eyes deepen. "Can't you try harder?

This is really important, April."

"Believe me, I wish it worked that way."

"We've got no leads." He motions in a semicircle toward the woods. "He could be anywhere out there. Or not in the woods at all."

"I know that," I say through gritted teeth. "Don't you understand? Gemma was my friend. You can't possibly know how bad this makes me feel that I can't help bring her son back to safety." Tears well in my eyes, and I rub my nose with the back of my hand. "I mean, all these years that I see stupid stuff that makes no sense or doesn't matter to me, but now that I can actually use it for some good. Can I? No. So quit looking at me with expectation."

"Excuse me," Buzz says.

Chase and I stop bickering and turn our attention to Buzz.

"We need to call this. It'll be dark soon, and I want to get all these volunteers back home. Everybody needs to dry off and get a meal in them. I sure don't want anybody catching their death of cold."

"What about tomorrow?" Chase asks.

Buzz rolls his shoulder. "The National Guard promises us two choppers. We're going to see if there is anything we can see from the air. But because of the proximity of Stephen when he was shot, this was our best opportunity. There is no telling where that little boy is right now."

I can tell Chase wants to argue the point. But what Buzz said makes perfect sense. We can search all of Marshall County, but it will do little to no good.

From the location of the stuffed bear, it is apparent that Jaxx was in the vicinity at one time. Nobody knows where Stephen took him after that, and Stephen can't tell us anymore.

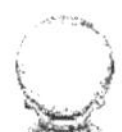    

I climb into Chase's pickup truck. The rest of the search party vehicles file onto the logging road. I give Chase his time, but when we are the last truck and the sun has begun to set, I ask him, "What are you thinking?"

"I don't understand. If you found Jaxx's stuffed toy, he had to have been near that house."

I nod. "Right."

"But Stephen was killed without Jaxx just a few hundred yards up the trail from the clearing where his truck was parked. So, if the bear was out by that abandoned home, Jaxx should still be up there."

"That would make perfect sense, Chase. Except we tore the place apart for an hour. He is not out there."

Chase turns his hands over in frustration. "But the toy. Why was it out there if Jaxx isn't?"

"Maybe Stephen put it there to confuse us."

Chase shakes his head vehemently. "No. He had no reason to go through the trouble, especially not with the storm brewing. It's not adding up."

"Maybe, but then again, you're trying to apply logic to somebody who believed it made sense to kill his ex-wife to gain custody of a five-year-old that he then put in danger."

"I suppose that is true."

I take a deep breath and blow it out in an exasperated puff. "You know something else that's true?"

"What's that?"

"I'm starving, and I think I'm starting to get a rash on my butt."

Chase tucks his chin against his chest and chuckles. "You kill me, April."

We are pulling into our parents' driveway when Uncle Howard calls.

Chase answers on his truck's Bluetooth. "Hey, Uncle Howard."

"How's your day, young man?"

"Honestly, I've had better."

"Aww, I'm sorry. I was hoping you would finish in first place today. I figure nobody knows the lake like you do."

"Yeah, actually, we never made it onto the water today."

After a moment of silence, Howard asks, "Are the two of you alright?"

Chase allows a tired-sounding chuckle to escape him. "That would definitely be a study in relativity."

"Hmm ... Sometimes relativity is simply a matter of changing your perspective, and other times it's a matter of adjusting your circumstances. Would a steak dinner and a couple of beers at Black Angus change your perspective? It might do you some good to unload your baggage. I'm a trained listener."

A tightness grips my chest as I see my brother grin. The last thing I need right now is a night out. All I want is to shower, devour half a gallon of pralines and cream ice cream, and curl up into a ball to feel sorry for myself. I am beyond physical and emotional exhaustion.

"Yeah, that actually sounds really nice."

I wave frantically to get Chase's attention. He finally looks at me, and his eyebrows push together as he watches me shake my head side to side, mouthing “no.”

He shrugs and mouths “why” back to me.

"I'm too tired," I hiss in a whisper back at my brother.

He rolls his eyes with a shake of his head. "What time do you want to get together?"

"Do you think you two can be out there at 7:30?"

"Yes, sir. That'll work."

"Good deal. I'm looking forward to it. Oh, and April?”

My eyes open wider. "Yes, sir?"

"Young lady, you are in the prime of your youth. The last thing you should ever be is too tired for a night out."

Fair. Howard's sage comment deserves an answer, but I am too embarrassed and flustered to muster a remark.

"All right, you two be safe, and I'll see you in a bit."

Chase disconnects the call and glares at me. "What is with you, anyway?"

Could it be the stress from a fruitless day of searching for a kidnapped little boy, the paranormal events from last night, or my overall physical discomfort? My ire bubbles over, and my "redneck" is out before I can catch her by the hair. "What's wrong with me? What's wrong with me is your constant expectation that I'm supposed to drop everything and do whatever Chase needs to be done. And then, on top of that, you have this harebrained idea that I have some sort of on-demand psychic ability to give the police clues about murders and stuff. I mean, my gosh, Chase. That's not how these things work. And it kills me to see you sulking because I can't do what you expect me to do."

I run out of things to spew and stop talking. My heart rate is up, and I'm forced to suck in another breath. Great, Chase is squinting at me as if a crazy woman dropped into the passenger seat of his pickup truck.

"I meant, how can you turn down a free steak from Black Angus?" He waves two fingers in the air. "All that other stuff. *No*. I don't know what it's about. I didn't earn it, so I'm not going to own it."

I would never admit it to either of them, but Howard and Chase knew what I needed tonight. I got my shower after all. But instead of empty calories from a tub of ice cream, I was treated to a mouthwatering filet mignon wrapped in bacon and a loaded baked potato. I ordered Italian dressing on my side salad rather than my usual ranch. After all, I'm counting calories.

Howard wasn't kidding about being a good listener. He always has been; I only forgot.

Like my daddy, he imparts a feeling of calm to situations that feel like they are irreparably off the rail. Often, they impart a bit of wisdom or offer another angle to look at a complicated crisis so that it becomes tenable.

There is no way to sugarcoat the situation with Jaxx. Howard agrees with Chase's and my fear. Every hour that passes, it becomes less likely that the police will find the little boy and return him to his aunt. Still, he insists that in dire situations, what is essential is everyone offers all the skills they have to their neighbors. To be a good neighbor, it is incumbent upon us to lend a helping hand to the best of our ability. After that, it is in God's hands.

Not to make everything about me, but I can't help but feel incriminated during our conversation.

Had I done everything I could? Why can't I call up the psychic portion of my "gifts" and lend some clarity to the situation for the authorities? A few years ago, I could touch items, like Jaxx's Winnie-the-Pooh bear, and get detailed color images, sometimes even owners' memories of notable events.

Shortly before I left for college, Nana Hirsch implored me to allow her to train me in my natural skills. She wasn't the only one. Granny also had dropped hints that it would be best if I spent time with her so she could explain what she learned from her career with the church before having her sons.

Nana commented that to develop and strengthen my "gifts" and gain operational control over them, I must practice them consistently at every opportunity. I understood her intent. She believed if I spent the summer with her before I went to college, I would master my "gifts" and not be forced to block them out. She did not want me relying solely on the mental partitions she taught me how to build in my mind.

I gleaned a different truth from her statement. To strengthen my "gifts," I needed to practice them regularly. If that is true, it doesn't take a Mensa member to understand that the converse must also be true. If I don't use my paranormal skills, they should atrophy and disappear.

In my heart, I never fully believed I would be completely rid of the abilities. Yet now, save for when I return to Guntersville for visits, the paranormal affliction that I suffer is a mere five percent of what it was when I left home. This gives me hope that sometime in the future, they will disappear altogether.

Today I could have really used those gifts I squandered. I could have saved the life of a friend's son.

"So, y'all headin' out in the morning?"

Chase shrugs. "Doesn't seem to be much point in it now. There is no chance of winning anything when everybody else is a day ahead of us."

"True," Howard agrees. "But if the tournament is successful, it'll be back next year. The experience of being in a qualifying tourney for the Bassmaster can't be bad. Plus, a little fishing might do both of you some good."

I don't mean to snort. It just sort of happens. "Sorry." My face feels red-hot.

Chase looks from me to Howard and back to me. "Would you still be game?"

After my rude gesture, I'd be a complete jerk to say no now. "It's what I came up for. If you want to go, I'll go."

Chase purses his lips as his brow furrows. "Yeah. I think I'd like to if you don't mind."

"I don't mind." Bless it. I assumed I would hang at the house tomorrow and then head back to Tuscaloosa a day early. I force a smile to reassure my brother that I don't mind.

"So, April. Are you still planning on going to work for Wee, Cheatham, and Howe?" Howard asks.

It's Chase's turn to snort. I cut my eyes to him and frown. He at least has the manners to look chagrined.

"It's Master, Lloyd, and Johnson," I correct my uncle.

"I was referring to their reputation, dear."

The sparkle in his eye and the smirk on his face reminds me of Daddy when he is poking fun at me. My uncle is four years older than Daddy. They are identical in height and broad build. Still, Howard carries an extra forty pounds and a lot less hair, which he attempts to make up for with an ineffective comb-over.

"Well, maybe I'll bring a little class to the joint," I smart back.

"You'll definitely add class. Unfortunately, I don't think that will do anything for their ethical issues."

I shake my head. "That is all rumors. I've researched those allegations thoroughly. There is no merit to them."

Howard puts his napkin on his plate and leans back. "Still, where there is smoke—" —"

"There are jealous people spreading misinformation," I say.

Howard grins, nods his head, and says, "Or people blinded by the smoke."

"How about some cheesecake?" Chase interjects.

Howard and I ignore him. We've entered into a game of stare-off. A game I excel at.

"All I'm saying, April, is that you are a highly ethical person, and firms like that push out people who don't want to play their dirty games.

"You've got a ready-made practice right here in your hometown, where people know and love you. You could make a good living while helping your community, and never have to compromise your morals. I've been planning my retirement for a long time. I don't even need any compensation, only the peace of mind that the business will be managed the way I have always tried to do business."

The fact that everybody knows me in this town is not an advantage. It's one of the reasons why I want to leave. That and to make the big bucks and make the seven years of sacrifice at the University of Alabama pay off, I need to be in a big market. Not some Podunk, North Alabama, town that people outside of Alabama can't pronounce correctly, much less use an interstate to drive to.

"Thank you for the offer. It's very generous of you. But you know I've always wanted to move to Atlanta. It's something I have to do."

"Cheesecake to go at least?" Chase asks.

As we walk out of Black Angus, Howard says, "Chase, can you give April and me a second?"

Chase looks at me, and I hand him our cheesecakes. He shrugs and continues toward his truck to wait for me.

"Look, all kidding aside. Master, Lloyd, and Johnson is a ruthless bunch."

I bow up and open my mouth to argue. Howard stops me by raising his hand.

"April, I've been following a journalist who's been doing investigative reporting on Master, Lloyd, and Johnson. A major investigation launched by the FBI centers on the three partners. I will forward you an advance release of the information for you to review. You must understand that this isn't about some old man who wants to give his niece his practice and ride off into the sunset. As attractive as that is to me, I know that your dreams are to establish yourself in a major market, and your dreams are important and valid, and you need to follow them. But not with these people. As your uncle, and more importantly, an uncle in the same profession, I can't allow you to go into that den of lions unprepared. Let me help you find another firm."

I understand that everyone is trying to help me. But I didn't ask for any help, and I don't feel I need it. I tilt my head to the left. "If I promise to read the information, will you let it drop?"

He exhales through his nose. His eyes soften, giving him a defeated appearance. "Do I have a choice?"

"No. You said your piece, and I promise I'll read the article. After that, it's on me."

"I suppose it is. But promise me that you'll remember, if things do go bad, I'm always here to help."

"I know and I do appreciate that."

"All right." He gives me a quick hug. "Knock 'em dead, kiddo."

"You know I will."

I watch my uncle walk to his ancient Volvo. As he backs out of the lot and pulls away, the first doubts about my new company tickle the back of my brain. I shouldn't let Howard get into my head like that. Master, Lloyd, and Johnson didn't become a super-regional powerhouse firm through unethical dealings. Everyone knows you don't get to their size with illegal activity.

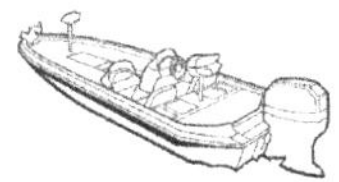

Chapter 10

For the second day in a row, I wake up to Chase looming over my bed. At least today is much better. After the heavy meal at Black Angus, I slept as if I were in a coma. Thankfully there were no dreams about abandoned houses, freaky dead deer, or visits from a ghost lady with a glowing purple necklace.

Being the early riser, Chase made us a breakfast of cheesy scrambled eggs, hash browns, and bacon. Although I'm not particularly hungry, I rarely get a breakfast like this unless I go to Waffle House. I won't let this special treat go to waste.

"That was another bad storm last night," Chase says in between bites of his bacon.

"Really? I must have slept through it."

"It was at least three times worse than the night before. The wind was really whipping."

My thoughts go to Jaxx. I wonder if he is still alive, and if so, I pray he was out of the elements last night.

I push the thought as far away as I can. I wish I had been able to do something for Jaxx, but as Grandpa Snow used to say, "It is what it is."

"I thought we should head over to the dam first," Chase says.

"That's stupid." I freeze with my bacon halfway to my lips, pausing to see if I said my thought aloud.

Chase frowns. "Why do you say that?"

Darn it. I hate when I blurt out my thoughts. It's as if my filter is broken.

"Isn't that where everyone who doesn't know this lake will try first?"

Chase wrinkles his brow in thought. "You know. You make a good point. Now that you mention it, I think we should ride over to the peninsula where the Ramseys built Eagles Point. The water is shallow in front of their dock, but there is a steep drop-off once you get fifty yards past the peninsula's tip. The channel is a hundred feet deep in that crease. We can pull some nice ones out of there on cool mornings."

Chase lifts his coffee mug and gestures toward me as he winks. "Thanks, Tink. That is a solid plan."

I smile down at my plate as my ears warm. "I'm always happy to be of service."

"You know, I don't care what Dusty says. You're a darn good angler."

I laugh. "The funny thing is, I don't care what Dusty says either."

Chase starts the boat motor. I untie us and step onto the boat while holding the line. Chase is mindful of letting me sit down on the bench seat before he throttles us into reverse, sliding smoothly out of the boathouse.

A thick, wet fog blankets the surface of our inlet. Visibility is fifty feet, tops. Not excellent conditions, but we've ventured out onto the water in much worse weather before.

I pull my hoodie up and tighten the drawstring, attempting to keep the dampness out of my hair. Today is not about how I look. It's about staying as comfortable as possible to hold my complaints to a minimum. This will be easier to accomplish if I'm not soaking wet and freezing.

Chase is back to his usual "be prepared" Boy Scout ways, and I am grateful. We have two coolers. One is full of bottled waters and Cokes, and the other is packed with sandwiches, chips, and apples. I suppose the apples are for Chase.

Either way, I know I won't be hungry or thirsty.

Finding the silver lining in the cloud, no pun intended, at least we won't be baking in the sun today. The day's high temperature is forecasted to be sixty, and it's supposed to be overcast all day. Perfect hoodie weather.

Easy peasy. Eight hours of casting with a few prerequisite snack breaks, and I'll get my "great sister" certificate for the year. If I get lucky and bring in a couple of largemouth bass, I might win the "best sister ever" trophy.

The idea of doing well today and seeing Chase pleased with me, as opposed to yesterday's disappointment, makes me square my shoulders for the task at hand. I want to earn my way back into his favored column.

We slide through the no-wake zone by the yacht club at the mouth of our inlet. The large lake houses that I know to be on our left are concealed by the fog. We're close enough to the club that I can make out a couple of the large yachts on the perimeter of their marina.

As my eyes scan from the yacht on our right back to the hill where the houses should be on the left, I see something dark floating in the water. "There," I say loud enough to be heard over the motor as I point.

"Got it," Chase says as he eases the boat to the right.

The item floating in the water passes on our left. It's a sizable branch that could have damaged our hull if taken at speed. At our present idle speed, it could still foul a propeller.

"I told you that storm was bad," Chase says.

Personally, I'm grateful I slept through it. Especially if there was any lightning illuminating my room.

The best thing about sound sleep is that if there happened to be a ghost lady watching over me last night, I was unaware of her presence. What I don't see can't scare me.

We near the buoys marking the entrance of our inlet. Chase gradually pulls the throttle back.

Sure, I might gripe about going fishing. But I can't deny the fact that I am a water girl.

Boat rides get me off. There is something about the anticipation building inside me the moment before the throttle is pulled back, and the noise of the boat shoots up that gets my blood pumping in expectation of the speed.

This morning the prospect of excitement is tempered by my concern that Chase is, by nature, a speed demon. I like to go fast, but Chase aims to go too fast.

The tip of the bow breaks the plane between the two buoys. Chase yanks the throttle back.

Adrenaline floods my bloodstream, and my body tingles as the nose of the boat lifts into the air. The invisible arms of momentum pull me back, pressing me into the cushioned bench.

The nose of the boat levels as we pass the small island to the left of the inlet entrance. The boat's hull skips sideways as Chase cuts hard to the left, too close to the island for my comfort.

We clear the side of the island and alarm four ducks into taking flight. We're traveling so quickly that the duck in the rear barely stays in front of us. As the duck gains momentum, he cuts to the right of our path to be rid of us.

My concerns about Chase's need for speed on days he is agitated are well-founded. Once we are level and moving in a straight line in the channel, he eases the throttle back. The hull lifts further out of the water. The sensation is that we are flying rather than skipping along the calm lake water.

I hoped that the fog would be less in the channel. It is, yet with the reckless speed Chase is traveling, it has not cleared enough for my liking. I pull my hoodie tighter around my face and press my chin to my chest. My face is now wet with mist from the low clouds and the occasional spray from the bow.

I could ask Chase to ease up. After all, we are already out of the tournament running.

But I know it has nothing to do with Chase's competitive nature. Instead, it's about taking something to the edge and still feeling like he remains in control. I get it. I like to control my environment, too. There is no peace for me when I don't feel in command of the things that impact my life.

Yesterday was a harsh lesson that we rarely govern our environment. No matter how eager the search team was to find Jaxx yesterday, and no matter how thorough the job we did, in the end, we controlled nothing. We were soundly defeated.

We had lost the game before we ever took the field.

So, I'll let my brother work off his frustration. Speed is an excellent antidote to shake off the blues when we are reminded we are only human.

The breakneck pace normalizes in my mind, and despite the wet chill of air blasting by me, I straighten my back and put my face directly to the wind. The water stings my face, and I grin as my wild-girl personality comes front and center, stretching her arms high above her head after her deep slumber.

Brave is one of the first words I would use to describe anyone in my extended family. Whether it's my brothers, my parents, or even my grandmothers, they seem to revel in all things problematic and dangerous.

Sometimes I assume I was adopted.

I'm a much more cautious person. Where being courageous is second nature to my family, I must practice and work at it.

But when I am, it is its own special kind of reward. I'm glad Chase is working off his soreness about yesterday's loss by speeding this morning. It feels wild and free. Also, even though I know the boat can go this fast, I know *I* will never drive the boat to this speed.

My heartbeat slows as the adrenaline wanes from my bloodstream.

I have missed being able to take a boat ride at a moment's notice with my family. It is something they still do often.

Of course, after I pay my dues in Atlanta and become a partner, I can get my own weekend lake home. Then I'll be able to go on a boat ride anytime I want to.

The sun cuts a hole through the fog and illuminates our boat like magic, Chase reaches to his right and pulls out a pair of cheap sunglasses. It tickles me as I watch him struggle to put them on while the boat jostles up and down.

The reflection of the sun makes his golden-blond hair glitter. The sparkle of his hair reminds me of when he was twelve, and Daddy allowed him to get a spiked Mohawk one summer. I thought it was tough. Mama thought it was an abomination and was madder than a wet hen at Daddy.

Dusty was just jealous. I think he knew he couldn't pull off the Mohawk look with his curly red hair.

Geez, we are getting so old.

Chase takes an unexpected sweeping right turn into an inlet. I struggle to stand and grab hold of the console as I put my other hand on his back.

"I thought you said we were going to Eagle Point," I yell over the engine's roar and rush of air.

Turning to me, he says, "Something is telling me to go toward the preserve."

Odd. I've heard Chase complain numerous times about the dearth of fish over by the preserve. Instead of catching fish, we're more likely to wind copious amounts of lake grass around his propeller and be cleaning his boat for the rest of the weekend.

Not that I care. It'll add fifteen minutes to the boat trip, which means, all told, thirty minutes less time available to cast. I'm sure Chase wouldn't make this decision if we were still in the competition.

The sun cuts a brighter hole through the fog. It's as if six separate light beams have burned a tunnel through the thick cloud canopy. Separated, they reach the dark lake surface, creating small islands of light in an otherwise dreary lakescape. The beams reflect like a mirror off the water, the glare forcing me to put my arm up to shield my eyes.

I see Chase lift his hand in my periphery and use it as a visor over his sunglasses.

The boat stops.

I fly forward, somersaulting and striking the front fishing

seat.

An impact knocks the wind out of me.

I hit the water? How am I in the water?

My hands and feet won't respond. My eyes refuse to open, and everything in my brain is a jumbled mess.

I suck in a breath, stop, and cough when it's water, not air. My mind dims, and my body doesn't respond to my commands.

I'm so tired. My head hurts.

The downward floating sensation calms my panic. The coolness of the water intensifies against my still body.

The dominant sensation is my blood throbbing a perpetual beat against my eardrums as the pressure from the lake water builds against them.

A hand latches onto my ankle, and a thousand pricks ignite under its grasp. I suppose the old man in the lake got me after all.

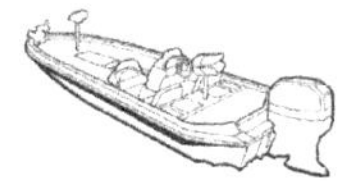

Chapter 11

Tony Joe White is singing "Polk Salad Annie."

Down in Louisiana, where the alligators grow so mean, there lived a girl that I swear to the world made the alligators look tame.

I love that song, and that is my favorite line. When I was little, and Nana would cook up a mess of poke salad, she would play the song for me.

Annie was dealt a bad hand in life, but she was a survivor. I respect that and aspire to have a hard edge like Annie. My edges are soft and rounded.

As for Nana's poke salad, I never tasted it. Mama told me that it's poisonous if it isn't cooked correctly. Nana is scary enough that I always wondered if I might have done something to anger her recently, and she might want to *accidentally* off me.

I have no idea why Nana has such an unsettling effect on me. The fact that she is an unrepented witch might play some small part in my prejudices.

Blast it. The entire room is filling up with the stench of the greens. I'm about to gag.

I grimace and turn my head to the side.

"Oh my gosh, she lives!"

The male voice booms, causing my head to throb. I open my right eye, and Chase grins like a loon in my face. I open my left eye and see the bowl of boiled cabbage he holds below my nose.

I arch my back and push away from the bowl as I struggle not to upchuck. "Oh, please get that out of here."

"Sorry. I thought you would be hungry." Chase looks over his shoulder. "Benjamin, come look. She is awake."

Chase stands and steps back from me.

"What happened?" I ask.

"I'll tell you in a minute. But let Benjamin check you out first."

"Hi, Ms. Snow. I'm Benjamin Cassidy, your nurse. If you allow me, I'd like to check you for a concussion now that you are awake."

I try to look around Benjamin to see Chase. It's apparent something happened to me.

Benjamin smiles, causing creases at the edge of his soulful dark eyes. "I promise it won't take but a second, and then I'll let you catch up with your brother."

It sounds like a square deal, and the presence of Benjamin makes me feel warm and happy. I favor him a nod as I lie back and try to relax.

He pulls out a penlight and checks my pupils. He writes something on his clipboard as he asks permission to touch the base of my neck.

Benjamin asks questions about my pain level as he touches various parts of my neck, and I respond. Still, I focus on how his large hands seemingly pull the pain out of the cramped vertebrae in my neck.

Benjamin writes more notes on his clipboard and smiles at me. "Have you ever considered taking up stunt doubling as a career, Ms. Snow?"

I squint my eyes. "Pardon?"

He laughs in a deep, pleasing baritone. "I'm only teasing you. My point being, given the event, I'm surprised"—he looks to Chase and back to me—"that you two will live to ride again. Y'all certainly can take a beating and keep on ticking."

"What happened?"

Benjamin gestures toward Chase. "I'll let your brother fill you in on the details. I can tell you that you're extremely fortunate, and I'm glad you are back with us. I'm on duty for another three hours. If you need anything, hit the little button there next to your pillow."

My eyes follow to where Benjamin gestures. I must be moving slowly. When I turn back, he is halfway to the door. "Thank you."

He stops, winks at me, and ducks out the door.

I turn my attention to my brother. "What happened?"

"What do you remember?" Chase asks.

His evasion causes a spike of aggravation because I don't remember anything. "Just tell me."

Chase retakes his position on the rolling stool at the side of my bed. "You know how there was a bad storm Thursday night?"

I nod in agreement. But I don't remember the storm.

Chase runs his hands through his hair. "I'm sorry. It's my fault. I never should have been driving the boat at that speed, given we had already seen obstacles in the water."

My eyes open wide as I remember the terrible tingle on my ankle when the old man in the lake grabbed hold of me. But how am I here?

"So, we crashed the boat, your boat?"

Chase frowns. "No, *I* crashed the boat. Between the fog and the sudden glare from the sun cutting through the clouds, I knew better than to continue at that speed. Even so, you should see what we hit, April. It looked like the trunk of a fifty-year-old oak tree."

"Your boat?"

Chase grunts. "The impact destroyed the hull. It all happened so fast I didn't have time to grab either of us a life vest."

My brother stares at me so long it makes me uncomfortable. He rubs the heavy stubble on his cleft chin. "I thought I lost you, Tinkerbell. You dropped below the waterline, and I couldn't find you. It seemed like you were gone for an eternity, and I knew I had to find you soon." He swipes at his right eye, sniffles, and looks away.

He is uncharacteristically upset, and it scares me. "Come on now, you know you can't get rid of me that easy."

"For the record, I didn't save you. I pulled us both out of the water, but I never found you." He gestures upward with his hands. "You just suddenly popped up. I was running out of breath diving down looking for you, and if you hadn't come up then, I don't know what would have happened."

I think Benjamin might have been wrong. I must have a concussion because I can't seem to think straight. The last thing I remember was the old man from the lake grabbing my ankle and me giving myself up to my fate. So again, how am I here?

"I called all the family and let them know what happened. Dusty said he would be back tomorrow. Granny is on her way up here now."

Since Mama is not in town, I could use Granny's comfort. I am concerned about Dusty returning so soon when he only arrived in Miami. He needs to take care of his business and not worry about me. "Dusty shouldn't cut his trip short."

Chase narrows his eyes. "He isn't. He was scheduled to be gone two days."

I do the math in my head. "What time is it?"

"About six in the morning?"

I make a face at Chase, and he snorts. "It's Saturday morning. You have been out almost twenty-four hours."

Well, that is not cool. Yes, Benjamin had the right of it. If the boat was totaled, and I've been unconscious for a day, I have to count myself as one lucky girl.

"Help me. Please, Lord, somebody help me."

"Help you what?" I ask Chase.

"What?"

Does Benjamin need to check Chase for a concussion, too? "You said, 'Help me.' Help you what?"

Chase shakes his head, emitting a nervous laugh. "I didn't say anything, April."

"Yes, you—"—" Forget about it. If Chase wants to play games, I don't have the strength to mess with him right now.

"Since we're talking about things folks shouldn't be doing, you should be more careful with your jewelry. You know better than to wear expensive stuff on the boat. That is just asking for trouble."

I reach for my earlobes. "I only wore my zirconium studs, and they're still in."

Chase tilts his head and gives me his "really" stare.

"What?"

"I'm certainly not into jewelry, and I still think it's an impressive piece. Did you get it from Granny?"

My lips open, exposing my teeth. "What are you talking about?"

"I only assume that because it has that old—no, antique—look about it. I know Granny has several jewelry pieces with that same look about them downstairs in her vault." His eyes narrow. "She knows you have it. Right?"

I blow out an exasperated puff of air. "Perhaps I could answer you if you care to explain what the Dickens you are talking about."

"The necklace you were wearing when we went fishing."

I swear. Sometimes talking to Chase is enough to drive me plumb out of my mind. One minute he explains in excruciating detail how to improve the torque of a combustion engine, and the next minute he sounds like an imbecile. Despite the low-grade headache and the bruises on my thigh that feels like somebody whacked me with a baseball bat, I try to keep my composure and say very deliberately, "Chase, I wasn't wearing a necklace."

He rolls his eyes and pushes off my bed, riding the rolling stool to the far side of the room. Standing, he lifts something up from the counter and holds it toward me. "What's this?"

My breath catches as I see a sizeable multifaceted, blood-red stone in the center of the intricate sterling setting. It's not the same color amulet that the apparition from the lake wore the other night. The stone is a crimson color rather than the luminescent violet.

Chase examines the amulet in an exaggerated motion, swivels his face towards me, and forms an "O" with his lips. "My word.

This looks exactly like a necklace."

I try to hide my concern as my brain struggles to create a plausible explanation. "Darn, look at you, Chase. Nothing gets by you."

"*So*," he drawls.

"So what?" I gesture with my hands, palms up. "So, you have a necklace. I think it may be a tad feminine for you, but to each his own."

"Ha-ha. Seriously, did you get this from Granny?"

"I should be asking you the same question. I've never seen that necklace before in my life." At least not that exact one.

"She doesn't know you have it, does she. That is why you won't own up to it."

I close my eyes and focus on calming my breathing. "Chase, when would I have gone to Granny's to get a necklace. Assuming that is where that one came from."

He is quiet, and I swear I see smoke coming out of his ears as he thinks through the possible scenarios. "I was saying it looks like some of the old stuff Granny keeps locked away in the vault. I've never seen you wear anything like this before."

"Chase, it does not belong to me. I don't even understand why we are having this ignorant conversation over a necklace—and quit calling it that—it's an amulet —that you are holding. Bless it. This is the stupidest prank ever, Chase."

He smiles and nods. "Okay, I get it. This is 'mess with your brother's head' day."

"More like 'mess with your sister...'"

The pieces to the puzzle fall together for me in a sudden epiphany. That is the thing, typically, if I can get people to talk long enough, they give away their game. While I was out, I must have said something about the ghost lady with the purple necklace from the other night. I've been told occasionally that I talk in my sleep. When I'm distraught, I may even walk in my sleep. Usually to the refrigerator for an ice cream sandwich, but that is not the important part.

It's just like Chase to think it would be hilarious to have a necklace for when I wake up. Never mind the fact that he almost killed me yesterday morning. Where Chase is concerned, the motto "never let a good practical joke go to waste" rules the day.

I must admit, he had me going. If Chase had been able to match up the color to the brilliant violet I saw the other night, it may have been enough to throw me into panic mode.

"Regardless of what you say, I know what I saw."

Fine. He obviously went to significant effort to put this ruse together. I might as well let him play it out to the end. "And what did you see, Chase?"

He raises his eyebrows and speaks adamantly with his hands. "I was exhausted from treading water, bruised, and crying because I just knew you were dead. Then you popped up out of the water. I grabbed hold of you and swam to shore. But I kept seeing this odd purple glow. When we reached the bank, I pulled you out of the water—, and this"—he holds the amulet up—"was around your wrist."

I struggle to conceal my smile. "Chase, why would I wear that around my wrist?"

His jaw drops open. "I don't know. That is not even the point. I'm telling you what I saw. Maybe it came off when you hit the water, and your reflexes allowed you to catch it."

"Now, that would be impressive."

"You know what, since you're being such an ingrate, I wish I had thrown the neck—*amulet*—back into the lake."

I shrug. "You can throw it anywhere you want. I don't care. It's not mine."

He glares at me, and I know immediately what he is about to do. Chase is the one person I can read like a book in my family.

"Fine. I'm going to go get some juice, and you can keep yourself company." He tosses the amulet, underhanded, in my direction.

Because I predicted he would throw it at me, I catch the amulet. Unfortunately, there is an IV in my right arm, and the motion jerks the needle and restraining tape. I fight back the grimace of pain.

"Brat," he says as he opens the door.

"Jerk," I respond back. I grin as Chase leaves. He can't stand that I didn't fall for his sophomoric prank.

The room brightens, and the palm of my right hand suddenly heats up. My breath catches in the back of my throat as I look down. The amulet radiates a dazzling violet glow. I avert my eyes so I'm not blinded by its brilliance.

Chapter 12

Calm down, April. There must be a perfectly logical explanation. I only wish I could think of it.

My initial reaction is to throw the amulet across the room. I feel the need to get it as far away from me as possible.

But my paranormal "gifts" are surging, and they crave holding the beautiful jewelry. Couple that with my insatiable curiosity, and it makes it impossible for me to set the amulet aside before I develop a hypothesis that satisfies the questions in my mind.

I now realize that Chase isn't putting on some elaborate hoax. Somehow, I went into the lake after being thrown from the bass boat in the collision and came up with the ghost lady's amulet.

Okay, if I flex my mind and remain calm, I can accept that. As improbable as it seems.

Unfortunately, that leads to the next obvious question, which is how. And if I'm ever able to determine how—which I find highly unlikely—that will only lead to the question of why.

I have no clue what all this means. But the twisting sensations in my stomach I can trust. They tell me that whatever this amulet symbolizes, it's not good for me. I force myself to hook the sterling chain around the arm of my hospital bed and unclasp my hand. I immediately feel a loss as the stone swings free of my hand.

Slowly, the stone's glow dims as it returns to the crimson

color it was before I touched it. It's as if, when joined, there is a symbiotic connection between the amulet and me. My energies light up whatever is inside the stone. Likewise, it brings a surge to my supernatural "gifts."

Gifts I've been desperately trying to bury the past few years, I remind myself. After all the progress toward normal, the last thing I need to do is start playing with something that might increase those powers. Especially when I'm so close to realizing my goals.

I stare at the stone and lick my lips. There’s something about it. I just want—no, need—to touch it again.

Absolutely not. I know I've kept my head buried in the sand all these years when my grandmothers tried to talk to me about the “gifts” that run in our family. In many ways, I have always believed that if I don't listen to them, that makes their assertions wrong. Both seem to think I doubled up on disparate supernatural abilities that both bloodlines have passed down through the generations.

I may have always avoided their innuendos and conversations, but I have learned a few things. Like "gifts,” artifacts can be a blessing, and they can also be a curse.

There is no doubt the amulet I want to put around my neck has been imbued with powerful magic. Still, I don't know if it's good or evil magic, and that should be enough to convince me to leave it alone.

I will take a positive from it, though. The few seconds I held the magical artifact in my hand removed the ache from my bruised thighs and cleared the fogginess that was addling my brain. I would consider that to make the amulet good magic, but truthfully that doesn't indicate anything definitive.

If I don't get away from it soon, I know it is a matter of seconds before I touch the crimson stone and turn it violet again. A vision of one of my favorite tortured characters from Tolkien plays in my mind. If I were to put the amulet around my neck as I long to do, I would be as doomed as Gollum by the end of the day.

The decision is not as difficult as I think. I pull the IV out of my arm, wrap the sheet around me to cover my butt, and walk barefoot into the hallway.

The nurses' station is empty, and I don't see anyone down the corridor. That is good. I'll simply wait here until Chase returns, and I'll ask him to take the amulet with him. That'll get it safely out of my reach.

It occurs to me that what may have happened is what Granny calls manifestation. Her claim is that if the need is great enough and the prayer is adequately passionate, people can bring to them what they need the most.

Of course, I don't believe her. But I'd be lying if I said that through the years, I haven't experienced a few cases of coincidences where I needed something, and it suddenly appeared in my purse or in my car when I knew it did not exist there prior. Whether it be a pen to write something down with or a twenty-dollar bill. It was never anything too large, and nothing I couldn't explain away as me being the luckiest girl in the world. Of course, a magical necklace that has all the appearances of being a priceless artifact is a tad past the scope of finding a Jackson in your jean pocket.

That begs the obvious question of why a necklace? When we hit the tree and I was thrown from the boat, I know if I had wished for something—if I was afforded the time to think—I would have hoped for a life jacket, not a piece of jewelry.

For heaven's sake, this makes my head hurt, which compels me to want to touch the amulet again since it relieved my pain. Maybe I should try some caffeine instead.

I wander over to the nurses' station and circle to the other side of the hallway. I know sometimes they have soda machines on each floor. If I'm lucky, I can find a Dr. Pepper.

The trouble I get myself into trying to make my brothers happy... If Chase hadn't needed me, the worst thing that could have happened this weekend is me adding on another five pounds I would have to work off. Right now, I should be sprawled out on my sofa binge-watching some mindless serial TV that I won't remember next week.

I shouldn't be in a hospital struggling to keep my butt covered while I jones for a Dr. Pepper.

"Help me!"

The plea makes me turn. No one is in the hall.

"No, get away. Leave me alone!"

Snap. I realize the voice is in my head, of all the rotten luck. Something has brought the voices back.

Cruising down the hallway, I work on rebuilding the mental partitions in my mind. The accident must have opened my mind to the voices. I shudder, realizing that the only place that would be worse for me to have my defenses down than a hospital is a graveyard.

However, it is my lucky day. I find a fountain drink dispenser, and Dr. Pepper is one of the flavors. My attitude brightens immediately as I fill a styrofoam cup with ice and beautiful, fizzy, caramel-colored Dr. Pepper.

As I transport my treasure back to my room, I'm surprised at how long Chase has been gone. I must have really hurt his feelings.

I get it. Chase was already sore about the accident, and my not believing him about the necklace only compounded his emotional state.

Honestly, I'm surprised he is not in mourning. That bass boat was his baby. That must be a terrible loss for him.

I sit down on the edge of my bed and greedily suck the spicy sugar water through the straw. My eyelids close as I enjoy the experience.

"Please, don't. I beg you."

Oh, for Pete's sake. I must be out of practice protecting my mind from the voices.

"No!"

My mind is playing tricks on me. This time the voice sounds like it's right behind me.

I slap my forehead with my fist. "La, la, la, la, la." I know that won't help, but it's worth trying, and I need the annoying voice to stop.

Surprisingly, it works. I don't hear anything anymore. Fantastic, I can enjoy my Dr. Pepper in peace.

While I nurse the drink in my hand, I struggle not to turn around and look at the amulet that I know is hanging off the side of the bed. I must jerk my head back twice to not look.

To make it more difficult to mess up, I turn so that the arm of the bed is directly behind me. I'm staring at the far corner of my room, which is boring, but I won't accidentally look at the jewelry. I swear I can feel the vibration of it warming my back. If I were to turn and look, I know I'd pick it up and wrap that beautiful sterling, endorphin-releasing serpentine chain around my neck. I'd rock that thirteenth-century bling like an empress.

I have a feeling that would be a monumental mistake.

My door swings open, and an athletic brunette in cranberry scrubs, who looks to be about the same age as me, enters. Our eyes lock. The woman squints and purses her lips.

"Why are you up?" she asks.

Forget the fact she is rude. I'm getting some high-intensity negative vibes from her. "I'm feeling better."

"I think the doctor will be the judge of that."

Her comment rubs my fur the wrong way, and I have half a mind to tell her off. She isn't worth the effort.

I roll my eyes and lie back down, making sure to tuck my right hand under my back so that I don't inadvertently touch my shiny precious dangling on the arm of the bed.

The nurse pulls the clipboard from the foot of my bed and does a cursory check of it. She looks up and follows my hand behind my back. I smile at her.

She tilts her head. "Aren't you supposed to have an IV in?"

"Maybe," I reply.

"It was rhetorical," she says as she grabs my forearm, pulling my hand out from behind my back.

Her fingernails bite into my forearm. Rage-filled emotions centered around desertion flow from her energy field to me.

I know I don't conceal my surprise at reading her because she stops and narrows her eyes.

"What?"

"Is Benjamin here?"

"No. You're stuck with me." She holds my arm and grabs the IV needle making to reinsert it. I'm not a nurse, but I would have thought I would get a fresh needle. I try to remain calm despite the torrent of negative emotions flowing from her. I look at her name tag to distract myself and keep me from clawing her eyes out for rolling my vein on the first try.

Peg. I should be able to remember that.

I collapse back onto my bed the second she releases me.

"If you pull that out again, it will become infected," Peg says.

No kidding. If you keep reusing the needle, I'll catch blood poisoning.

She shakes her head at me and exits my room. Her cloud of negativity remains in the room for a minute before clearing.

My "gifts" aren't always reliable, but something is up. Peg is not just a negative person. She is up to no good.

I consider touching the amulet. My arm hurts, and I would like to see if it might give me a vision of what Ms. Peg has up her scrubs. It's none of my business; still, I want to know.

Oh, stop it, April.

The probability of the amulet indicating the criminal intent of a stranger is low at best. It is more probable that I am trying to form a weak justification for holding the stone in my hand again.

So, Peg has the bedside manners of Hannibal Lecter. That doesn't make her an evil person. A terrible nurse and an angry woman, sure, but everyone can have an off day. Right?

It's hard to imagine this day going any worse. I'm backsliding on my powers, and now I've got this stupid piece of jewelry that I'm afraid to touch.

Where is Chase when I need him? I need him to put the amulet back on the counter and cover it up so I can't be tempted by its sight.

I try to center myself by closing my eyes and concentrating on organizing the energy around me. I can feel the presence of the amulet to my right. It's like being outside and feeling the sun on one side of my body and not the other.

There is a niggling feeling in my mind. I decide to act on it. If nothing else, it'll get me away from the amulet.

Not wanting to be stabbed a third time with the same needle, I grasp the IV holder toward the top of its stand and pull it behind me out into the hallway. Peg, the sadist, is nowhere to be seen.

I don't know what I expect to find, but I know whatever is bothering me is in the next room. I roll my IV stand in front of the room and tap lightly on the door. Nobody says anything.

I push the door halfway open. "Hello? Can I come in?"

Again, no answer. That is not necessarily a terrible thing.

I shuffle into the room, a mirror image of mine. Our headboards are separated by a six-inch-thick wall.

The patient in the room looks to be in terrible shape. His color is wrong, yellow with a green tint, and he remains unconscious.

Being optimistic, I can eliminate this room as a potential source of the voice I heard. This man is silent, and I don't feel any energy in the room.

I pull my IV stand along with me to the side of his bed to look at his face. He has a strong chin and a lovely, aquiline nose. His shock of black hair needs to be washed. It's challenging to be positive, due to his odd sickly coloring, but he may have been handsome before becoming sick.

That is unfortunate. The patient doesn't appear incredibly old. Oh well, maybe he will snap back from whatever he has.

I shuffle and pull my way out of his room. Pulling the door closed behind me, I wonder if he is married and has children.

"What were you doing in there?" Peg says as she bolts from behind the nurses' station.

"I wanted a Coke, and I accidentally went into the wrong room." My face flushes hot. I am the world's worst liar.

Her lips tighten into a razor-thin red line as she stomps toward me. "I don't believe you."

She looks like she plans to throttle me. Usually, that wouldn't concern me much, except I have an IV still stuck in my arm, and

I'll be forced to rip it out before I can defend myself.

"Don't believe what?" Chase's broad back passes in front of me.

"Excuse me, I need to get my patient back to her room."

"She is my sister. I'll take care of it for you."

I can't see Peg due to the width of my brother's shoulders, but I sigh a breath of relief when I see Peg's white sneakers retreat from between my brother's legs.

Chase puts his left hand under my right arm and walks me back. "Making friends, as usual, I see."

I laugh and grimace as one of my ribs flares with pain. "Hush up."

Chase opens the door to my room. A five-foot-tall woman with an incredible bouffant hairdo of snow-white hair stands before me, holding the amulet. "Where did this come from?"

 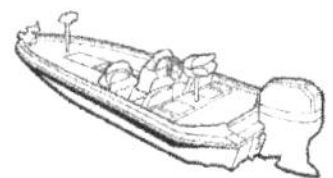

Chapter 13

Granny Snow is a diminutive woman by anyone's standard. Still, when she asks a pointed question, it always has the tendency to freeze me in my tracks like a small animal coming upon a hunter with a shotgun.

My mouth drops open as my eyes open wider. "Uh..." I quickly opt for self-preservation and gesture with my thumb toward Chase.

It doesn't have the desired effect of getting me out of Granny's crosshairs as Chase's face twists with anger. "You did take it from her collection," he accuses me.

"No, I didn't." I turn my attention back to Granny to plead my innocence. "I didn't even know you have a collection."

Her facial expression changes dramatically. I realize she is not angry; Granny is scared.

"What kind of collection is it?" The words escape me before I think of the consequences. If I'm ever to be rid of my paranormal affliction, the sooner I quit being in the weird world of my grandmother's mumbo-jumbo reality, the better.

Granny frowns. "It's nothing you need concern yourself with, sweetie."

I notice something peculiar. I wish I didn't. Despite all her purported abilities, the amulet remains its crimson color in Granny's hand. It does not cast its eerie violet glow as she clutches it.

Something different about my touch coaxes the strange light from the artifact. Perhaps the power is from my maternal grandmother's side of the family. The thought sends me into a shudder as a chill slides up my spine.

"I would like to know when you first saw this," Granny says.

I pull the scratchy hospital sheet tighter around my chest. "When I woke up."

A hint of a smile graces Granny's face.

"I first saw it when I pulled us to shore after the accident," Chase interjects. "It was wrapped around her wrist. I hadn't noticed her wearing it when we shoved off."

Granny's complexion grays as her eyelids twitch. "You are positive you didn't find this somewhere else and put it on, April? Maybe in your father's stuff."

"My father's stuff?"

Granny closes her eyes, drawing in a long breath. "This is important. I must find an explanation. You two took a hard tumble on the water. Perhaps you found this amulet in Ralph's office and thought you'd wear it? Maybe after taking the nasty blow to your head and almost drowning, you forgot you had it on?"

I snort. "Right. Daddy keeps a collection of women's jewelry. That wouldn't be weird in the least. Not to mention if I did find something like that"—I point at the red stone in her hand—"I don't think it's an appropriate accessory for a bass tournament."

My shoulders creep up toward my earlobes. I fully expect Granny to put me in my place for smarting off. "Okay."

Okay? Are you kidding me? I've never been able to smart off to Granny.

"But, Granny. She had a hoodie on when we hit the tree. The impact can't have torn the amulet off her neck from under the hoodie." Chase wrinkles his brow. "If she wore it on the boat and I didn't notice her wearing it, she had to have it under her hoodie —but none of this makes any logical sense."

Granny tucks the amulet into her pocket. "You're right, Chase.

But don't trouble your mind on the logic of things. Some things are beyond logic. In any event, I'll take this with me and find a place for it with my other things."

Her words "other things" cause me to flinch. Contrary to Chase's belief, Granny did not previously have the amulet in her collection of woo-woo items.

I'm salty about being the only person who didn't know she hoards magical items in a secret place at her home.

I really do fight to keep my question inside. "What aren't you telling me, Granny?"

She bites her upper lip as we stare at one another. She inadvertently scrapes the rosy red lipstick from her lip.

"Granny? Tell me."

Granny looks to Chase. "Chase, can you give us a minute?"

Suddenly I have the urge for my big brother to stay with us. "He can stay."

Chase waves his hand. "Nah. I'm good. I have the feeling this is about to take a turn toward one of y'all's ghost stories. That stuff gives me the willies even though I know there is no such thing as ghosts."

Chase squeezes my forearm as he goes behind me and leaves me alone with the curse of my birthright. The door taps shut behind me.

"April, you must stop being so conflicted in these matters."

"Conflicted about what, Granny?"

She emits a derisive laugh. "Your 'gifts.' You must decide if you're going to embrace them. Which requires you to learn what they are, where they come from, and, more importantly, how to harness them. You can't continue to put them aside, and when you become interested, dabble in them just enough to be dangerous. And I need to stress, not just hazardous to yourself, but everyone around you."

"I don't understand Nana and you. You're always talking in riddles, and I don't understand." I stomp my bare foot on the tiled floor. "How can I understand when nobody talks plainly."

Granny narrows her gaze when I mention Nana. It is an

understatement to say the two women do not see eye to eye. Granny always bristles when I bring Nana up in conversation.

"I can't speak for Pauline. I can tell you I don't want to involve you any more than you have to be since you have made it perfectly clear you have no intention of developing your talent. If you're not planning to master your God-given skills, you need to do like your brother and dismiss them entirely. You cannot keep one foot in the world of nonbelievers and the other in the world of those of us who acknowledge there is more to this world than what man's eye can see."

"It's not that simple, Granny," I whine. "I do want to be normal. I want to be a defense attorney, not some sort of freak."

"You're not a freak, April. Being blessed with spiritual sight is not a handicap. It is a gift meant to be utilized."

"I respectfully beg to differ. I hear stuff and see stuff that nobody should be sensing. And every time I think I'm getting better and I'm closing off from those unexplainable things, it all comes back in a mad rush."

"I've explained this to you before, April. The veil is exceptionally delicate with you. Possibly even torn."

"How do I fix it?" I lean forward and shake my arms in frustration. Pain radiates in my right forearm from the IV, and I grab hold of it.

Granny moves forward and cradles my elbow. I shake her off.

"Stop," I say.

"Let me see it."

Reluctantly, I give her my arm. She rubs her finger alongside the IV. "The needle is still in, but it looks irritated."

"I may have jostled it a few times today," I grumble.

Granny puts her hand on the small of my back as she holds my right arm. "Let's get you back in bed so it doesn't happen again."

"I want you to tell me what you are hiding from me. I want to hear about this place that everyone else in the family seems to know about where you keep stuff."

"I promise I will if you get back in bed."

Granny helps me back into bed, fusses over the sheet that she straightens, and brings it to my hip, where she carefully folds the edge before smoothing it. She offers me a smile. "Do you mind if I sit down in the recliner?"

"Sounds like a long story," I joke.

She makes her way over to the recliner and sighs as she sits. "Maybe not long, but one that taxes my soul greatly."

Her comment sobers me. I turn my full attention to her.

"April, there is a lot about our family that we've kept from you."

I nearly say, "No kidding." Thankfully I manage to hold the remark. Whatever Granny is about to tell me, I'm hungry to hear it.

"I believe in the beginning when you were born, and it was apparent you were "gifted," we buried our history. It scared us what it meant for you, and besides, you were a child. There would be an appropriate time to tell you when you were closer to adulthood. But with each birthday, it became easier to believe that there was no need to trouble you with our families' histories. We were especially relieved as you continued to voice your intent, loudly, that you planned to move from Guntersville as soon as you were old enough."

Granny pauses and crosses her legs. "In my years of service to the church, I never knew someone to be such an open conduit as you, to the other side of the veil. When you had the coming-of-age event and all your powers manifested in earnest, I couldn't help you." She sighs. "Only Pauline could offer you refuge by teaching you how to build the partition in your mind with her abominable magic. I'm grateful to your nana since none of my skills could offer you peace. It was my first lesson in accepting the anomaly of my only granddaughter. You are uniquely created with two powerful abilities never meant to mix."

It's never been made clear to me the differences in my grandmothers' abilities, so this is of interest to me. The only thing I do know is that they derive their powers from their disparate and adversarial religions. Granny from her Christian beliefs and Nana from her animist beliefs.

"I prayed you would learn her lessons and practice the skills well enough to allow you to become that which you sought most. To be 'normal,' as you say." She smiles. "Your family wants you to be happy. Still, after all these years of monitoring your progress, I must speak of something you don't want to hear. You will never be fully normal. You ask me how to fix your condition. I'm confident you will never be able to snuff out all the paranormal events. You're just too strong of a magnet to them."

Her words spook me to my core. "No. I'll be rid of them."

As I hear my words, I know they are false hope.

Granny stares at the floor. "This is the hardest thing for a grandmother to say. If you have any chance to be rid of the supernatural events, it will be far from here. The veil is not the same everywhere. In Guntersville, it is particularly stretched and fragile. That, and your family's past interwoven with the town's history, precludes anyone like you from finding peace here."

Tears well in my eyes. Not because Granny is telling me to never come home—I've been working diligently toward that goal for years—but she confirms what I have felt all along. When I'm in Guntersville, something is always watching me. I've never been able to identify it so, naturally, I couldn't talk about it to anyone else without sounding outhouse rat crazy. Who knows, maybe I am crazy.

Still, I have been unable to shake the feeling that in Guntersville, an unseen force is stalking me. An entity biding its time patiently as it plans how best to entrap me.

I hate the feeling. As much as I love being with my family, the constant threat in the back of my mind keeps me on perpetual alert. Home does not feel like a safe harbor to me. The people, my family, are, but the town is not.

"Of course—, that wouldn't be the case if you would allow me and Pauline to train you regarding your unique gifts."

"I don't want to..." She stops me by raising her hand.

"I know your feelings on this. And I'm not trying to change

your mind on the subject. I'm only reminding you there are other options besides leaving home. If you were to allow us to impart all that we know, you might be able to combat Guntersville's history." She shrugs. "Then again, maybe not."

I scoff. "If there is no guarantee, why would I?"

"Because there is no guarantee that you can put enough miles between you and here to rid yourself of your destiny. None of us know how long the reach of this area is for you. This is uncharted territory for all of us."

"You're not making me feel better."

"The times of saying things to make you believe everything will work out have long passed, April," she says with a frown. "For that, I am truly sorry."

Even if I don't want to hear that from Granny, I know she is right.

"So, what's with this top-secret storage facility you have?"

"You make it sound so superhero—ish," she says with a chuckle.

"Well?"

"Do you remember your grandpa's upstairs office?" she asks.

I do. I remember the bookshelf that runs along the right side of the room. Grandpa was an avid reader, and his collection was full of farming, herding techniques, and business books. He would let me sit with him while he did his accounting ledgers. The "books," as he called them.

We rarely spoke. Grandpa would work on his numbers while I read books well above my grade level. Yet it was my favorite sort of "visiting." We seemed to share so much by being in the same room, toiling silently at our task of choice.

"Yes, ma'am."

"Do you remember how you would remain with your grandpa in his office for hours during the summers when you came to stay?"

I smile as the scent of leather and butterscotch wafts to me, as if I were magically revisiting his office. Grandpa always kept a glass jar of butterscotch hard candies on his desk. I can't taste butterscotch without thinking of the tall, broad-shouldered and white-haired man who always made me feel safe. "Yes."

"The collection is in my room behind his desk. If you recall, there is a door directly behind his office chair."

There was a door. Grandpa told me that it was where he stored old files in case he was ever audited by the “G-men.” I knew he meant IRS, but G-men sounded exponentially more sinister.

I'm not sure why, but I found that as deviously hilarious then as I do now. My Grandpa, the straight arrow, rebel?

Granny squints. "Don't you ever find it odd that you always wanted to sit upstairs and watch your grandfather do the farm finances? You never found it strange that whenever his office was unlocked, you were attached to him as snuggly as his shadow?"

I have a sudden sense of falling. Like the floor of my known world collapsed, and I'm left clutching at anything to stop my fall. "I just liked sitting with him."

"Really?" She laughs. "A little girl wants to spend hours watching her grandfather do debits and credits?"

She is right. It doesn't make sense, but I'm not going to let logic stop me from trying to set my world back straight. "Well, I wasn't any good in the kitchen."

"April, honey," she drawls. "It had nothing to do with your abilities in the kitchen. The things in that room were calling to you. That is why you always had the itch to be up there."

A chill runs across my chest, and I shake it off. I know Granny is right. Still, this is not what I need to hear. "I just like butterscotch."

She appears to let me have that lie. She lifts her hip and pulls the amulet from her pocket.

I lick my lips and tuck my fingernails into the palms of my hands. Granny watches my reaction, and we exchange a knowing stare.

"This beauty, despite Chase's assumption, has never been in my collection," she says.

"But you have seen it before. I mean, you seem like you have."

"Yes." She leans back, holding the amulet to her chest. "I knew the woman who owned it last."

I lean toward her. "It's magical, isn't it?"

She raises her eyebrows.

I fear she will hold her secret, as Snows are so often known to do.

"Quite so. But the powers were specific to her. It would only come to life for her."

I freeze and make sure that I don't give away a tell-tale smile. I'm not prepared to let Granny know that the amulet lit up for me earlier. I'll have to take the chance that Chase omitted that bit of information when they discussed its sudden appearance from the lake.

"Is it good or bad magic?"

Granny rolls her eyes. "Oh, honey. That is like saying, is it a good or bad hammer. When a hammer is used to build someone's house, it's a good hammer. If you use it to crack someone over the head, it's a bad hammer.

"'Gifts' are the same as tools. It has more to do with who uses the tool and for what purpose than what the tool is."

"Was she good?"

"I feel she was. Her heart was good. But we're often influenced by the people around us. The people we love."

I become frustrated that Granny has broken into another case of riddles-r-us. "You keep talking about her in the past tense."

"Yes. Because she is no longer with us." Granny looks away from me. "I knew her when I was much younger. Way before you and your brothers were born."

"Y'all were tight?"

She flashes me a smile. "Very. She was incredibly special to me."

"What happened to her?"

"Is that really important? All that matters is that she is no longer here."

My hyper-curiosity can be so rude. "Still, what happened? Was it sudden?"

"Yes, and no. I knew she was hurting. The man she loved had broken her heart. I tried to help her see what he was, cruel at the least, but most likely evil. Like many of us, when we fall in love, she could not see her lover for who he really was. Even though I knew she was hurting, I never anticipated what she would do to herself. For that, I will stand convicted."

As I watch the dark expression settle on Granny's face, I see her as a person for the first time in my life. Not my grandmother, but another human being with the same self-doubts and guilt that I have.

"I'm sorry," I say.

"Me too. She was a beautiful soul. Loving, fun to be around, unfortunately highly attractive, so she drew the interests of all sorts of men." She laughs, but there is no humor in its tenor. "When Randolph appeared, she found him simply charming, and he was. He was handsome, seemed to have plenty of money, and doted on her incessantly.

"Still, my 'gifts' told me it was all an act. In time, unfortunately, my 'gifts' proved to be correct."

She pulls the amulet from her chest and holds it out. I long to run my fingers along the sterling serpentine chain and caress the blood-red stone back to its violet glow.

"This was supposed to be their pre-engagement gift. Soon after, she found she was with child. Then his true nature began to show. He insisted that she move in with him, which was totally against the belief system she had been raised in. Once she was in his home, he kept her stowed away from her family and friends. None of us were allowed to see her. *Ever*."

The fact Granny would allow one of her friends to be treated this way surprises me. I come from a lengthy line of people who stick their nose in other people's business when folks are being treated incorrectly. "What did you do?"

"She put us in a terrible position because we couldn't do anything. When we could get word to her, she would tell us that Randolph knew best and Randolph was taking care of her. She only talked of him as if she was a tape recorder on an endless loop. It was always ‘Randolph this’ and ‘Randolph that.’ Dionis would never concede he was anything other than perfect."

Granny tucks the amulet back into her pocket. "The baby was born. And it got worse."

She becomes silent and stares at the far wall at length. I can tell that whatever happened to Dionis tortures Granny, and I consider telling her I know enough. I don't want her to put herself through any more misery by recounting the event to me.

"I only wish that Dionis had talked to me about her depression beforehand. There were things we could have done."

Granny taps the bulge in her pocket. "I'm positive she used the magic from this to facilitate her death. When she came to the surface two days after we started the search, there was nothing to hold her to the bottom of the lake. Nothing at all."

She leans toward me and clasps her hands in front of her. "You understand that you can't walk out into the lake and sink for two days. That is not possible."

I understand the question to be rhetorical, and remain silent. There is nothing I can add via conversation as I attempt to wrap my mind around the story of Granny's friend.

"But the amulet wasn't with her. When she came to the surface, that is. But I knew. I knew that it was something magical that held her down long enough to take her life."

"The child?"

Granny rocks back and forth in the chair. "Randolph figured out pretty quick that he needed to leave. He abandoned his son. I considered raising the boy but knew that it would be best to get him far away from Guntersville, considering who his parents were. He was placed in foster care. I lost track of him after a few years."

My Granny is as lousy of a liar as I am. I notice the flesh of her cheeks and ears flush beet red, but I feel it best to let her have her white lie. There is no harm in a concerned friend keeping tabs on an orphaned child. It seems natural to me.

"You do understand what I'm saying about the amulet. It has been missing since Dionis killed herself."

I exhale and fall back onto my hospital bed. "It just goes to confirm what you say is true. I'm some sort of freakish supernatural magnet when I'm in Guntersville."

Granny stands and pats me on the shoulder. "It's okay. We'll help you get through this."

"I'm going to get through this because I'm moving to Atlanta," I say as I watch her digging through her purse.

"Remember that if it continues in Atlanta, it will be in your best interest to learn what you can from your grandmothers."

I disagree with her. I have had the best luck by staying as far from the craziness as possible.

Granny slides a picture out from her wallet. "I thought you might like to see a picture of Dionis."

Leaning forward, I steady Granny's hand holding the picture, which is shaking something terrible. I look at the beautiful woman in the image, and the room spins out of control.

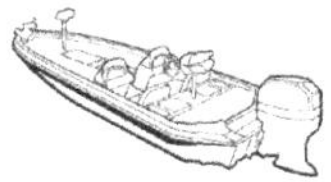

Chapter 14

I'm unprepared for this shock. Granny's Dionis is the shadowy lady from the lake. It's the face of the woman who was in my room the night of the thunderstorm.

"This picture was taken before Randolph came to town. In this picture, she looks happy. As I remember her," Granny says.

She does appear happier in the picture than she looked the other night when she visited my room. Of course, her being dead now may have soured her current disposition.

Granny pulls her hand away, sliding the picture back into her wallet. She arches her eyebrows. "You've seen her?"

My heart skips a beat. "No, ma'am."

"April May."

Ugh. My life would be so much easier if I had a poker face. "Maybe."

She shakes her head. "I showed you the picture for a reason. I already had my suspicions. Did you see her in the lake?"

"No. I mean, I think I saw her come out of the lake a few days ago. But I couldn't see her face then since it was dark outside. But later that night, she was in my room."

Granny makes a tsking noise. "This isn't good."

"Is she a witch or something?"

Granny's expression sours. "No. She was not a witch despite what Pauline says. She did, however, have some powerful spiritual abilities. The amulet that Randolph gave her somehow magnified those abilities. I think, secretly, he hoped to use her spiritual powers later to secure their fortune."

"She could do that?"

"She had the manifestation skill. Like mine, only more powerful, and with the amulet it was amplified." Granny watches as I'm about to ask another question. "I would explain further if you ever wanted to train yourself to use your skills properly."

She knows how to shut down my line of questioning.

"This is the first time her spirit has appeared since her death. We all assumed she had passed through the veil."

"Maybe she did. I can't be sure that what I saw matches that picture perfectly."

"And the amulet?" she asks.

Yeah, that one is sort of tough. "It was at the bottom of the lake, and I hit so hard my wrist went through the chain and got tangled?"

Granny shakes her head. "Now you're just reaching."

Yes, I am. But I don't feel like leaving things unanswered.

As we talk, Granny flits around the hospital room like a bumblebee. It's exhausting just watching her. "Are you leaving me?"

"Yes. I want to get this stored away as soon as possible."

"I didn't think it affected you."

Granny grins. "It doesn't. But your eyes keep going to my pocket. I feel it's time to get the temptation out of your reach."

That makes sense to me. Granny leans over the arm of my bed and gives me an extended hug. She favors me with another smile and walks out of the room.

I am thankful that she took the amulet with her. I would have liked to run my fingers over the serpentine chain once more and feel the amulet's weight against my sternum. Just imagining slipping the magical item over my neck makes me hum deliciously with power. It would be wonderful to wear it, even if only for a few seconds. What could that hurt?

I try my best to push the amulet business from my mind. I must focus on the last few weeks of law school. Then I'll need to consider the once-in-a-lifetime celebration party I'll throw myself for graduation. My impending party has been my favorite topic for the previous seven years and has kept me on task.

All I see is the multifaceted crimson gemstone. How I want to hold it in my hand again.

Where is Chase? It's one thing to give Granny and me privacy while we discuss the paranormal oddities of my life, but the least he could do is come back and distract me.

Chase is not nearly the conversationalist that Dusty is. Still, he could offer a welcome interruption from my obsession with the jewelry that magically attached to me in the lake.

"No!"

The plea is disorienting, and I survey my room. I drop my chin to my chest. Blast it. It's the stupid voice in my head again.

It's difficult to remember, partly because I naturally push terrible things from my memory and put an extra shine on the good stuff. It's been a decade since the worst afflictions of voices in my head, but it was dead people in the past.

No, I don't think there is any shortage of ghosts wandering the hospital. In fact, hospitals are only second to graveyards for roaming spirits. There may be a higher percentage of lingering ghosts at the hospitals since they attach themselves to the last place they see and remain disoriented and in denial of their death.

"Please have mercy, Peg."

The name Peg makes me sit up straighter. That is the name of my ill-tempered nurse. The one who looks like she is ready for the trainers to put Vaseline on her face right before an MMA bout.

"You're killing me, Peg."

Butterflies take flight as my stomach lurches. A tingle radiates between my shoulders while the hair on the back of my neck stands on end.

I'm not just rusty on how to build mental partitions. This plea is full of emotion. Whoever is making the cry for help believes they are in mortal danger.

I know better. It's the last thing I should be doing, considering I'm close to escaping my paranormal peculiarities.

I'll have my juris doctorate in ten short weeks and be busy studying for the bar at Master, Lloyd, and Johnson. I deserve my reward for a job well done.

The perfectly logical rationalization of why I should mind my own beeswax is ignored in the court of my conscience. Before I realize what I'm doing, I pull the random energy in the room inward and compress it at my sternum.

I could stop now. I should stop now and protect my future.

Instead, I take a deep breath and exhale slowly through my nose. Forcefully, I push the energy out as far as I can and hold onto its tail.

I discovered and mastered this skill when I was a little girl. When my brothers and I would play hide and seek, I hated when it was my turn to find them. My brothers were four years older and hard-core competitors who hid like highly trained military snipers. There was no hole too small, tree too high, or area too nasty for them to hide.

Quite by accident, I realized that I would get an odd itch in my chest when I was close to Dusty, my brother with a sprinkling of paranormal abilities. Over time, I harnessed the energy in the areas around me. I sent out "feelers" that helped me pinpoint things I was focusing on. Unfortunately, it also could identify paranormal and evil things in my path.

Frowning, I let the energy field loose when I sense the commotion is directly behind me. Again, it's the room with the unconscious man.

I wrestle with the decision of going to check on him again. I've already been in his room and found it void of energy.

But you just felt something now.

I fall back onto my pillows, punching my fists into the mattress. I frigging hate my life. Why can't I just be normal?

This is all making my head hurt. I just gave myself a migraine, too.

What is the deal? How can I keep hearing and feeling something behind me when the dude is all but dead with no energy imprint in his room? This makes absolutely no sense.

Where the heck is Chase? Did he get lost looking for a Payday candy bar or something?

Fine. I'll go check out the room a second time. I'm obviously not going to get a bit of rest until I solve this mystery.

I slide my legs gingerly off the bed, making sure not to jostle my IV again. I wrap my sheet around me and pad over to my door.

Peeking my head into the hallway, I see I am clear of Peg.

Carefully, I slink along the railed wall, skillfully quiet like a professional cat burglar, yet dragging a squeaky-wheeled IV stand behind me.

It occurs to me that this obsession of mine is getting a little out of hand. This must be the last time I check on the room behind me.

Something I haven't considered before is I may have a concussion. There may be no voice in the room behind me. It may be my poor scrambled brain uttering remnants of past conversations.

I've never had a concussion before. At least not diagnosed. I come from an extensive line of hardheaded Southern people known to be able to take a punch. So, it does come as a bit of a surprise that I might have experienced one. Then again, I've never been involved in a high-speed boat accident either.

I don't bother to knock on the door this time. I know the nearly dead, attractive man wouldn't answer anyway.

"You think you're better than me. I'm not some soiled Kleenex you can throw in the garbage after you pleasured yourself. I'm a human being."

I freeze in place as I attempt to discern if that voice is in my head or the room. I'm praying it is in my head because it's the voice of an unstable woman.

"All those times I listened to your lies. Now it's your turn to listen to me. But I won't ever lie to you, that I can promise. So, listen up. You will never leave this bed. At least not until they wheel you down to the autopsy room."

My temples throb. Probably because I sucked in my last breath of air thirty seconds ago, and I need to breathe. I'm afraid Peg, I recognize her voice now, might hear me.

A multitude of thoughts swirl through my mind. Some helpful, like the inclination to slide back out the door, which my feet won't abide. Other ideas are random, like will I be awarded my juris doctorate posthumously if something happens to me.

Peg circles around the foot of the bed. She jerks her head when she notices me in the doorway.

"What are you doing?"

My eyes open wider as my jaw drops open. I make a guttural sound from my throat. "Uh—"—"

Her eyes narrow as she approaches me. "How long have you been there?"

I have a brain lock, and I flush hot all over. I know if I don't come up with something quick, my goose is cooked. Cooked, that's it. I gesture with my thumb over my shoulder to the door. "I didn't see you at the desk, and I wondered when lunch is served."

She eyes me suspiciously. I believe there is still a chance she may attack me. The thought makes me swallow hard. She looks like she would be a good fighter, and I've never had to defend myself half-dressed—with an IV in my arm.

"You can't be going into other patients' rooms. It's against hospital regulations. It's how deadly diseases are transmitted through hospitals," she scolds.

Without thinking, I crane my head and look at the man on the bed. "What's he got?"

"Cerebral hemorrhage, if you must know," she hisses.

I want to bring up the truth that neither cerebral hemorrhage nor concussions are transmittable. When Peg grasps my arm with her hand, the flood of anger and humiliation forces me to wisely omit that discussion.

"Let's get you back in bed."

"And lunch?" I think it best to continue to sell my weak alibi.

"Soon, but I can bring you a snack if you want."

I consider what might be in the snack she is offering me. "Please don't trouble yourself. I'm sure I can wait. Besides, I don't want to spoil my appetite."

This lying thing gets easier the more you practice it. I'm relatively proud that I think Peg bought that last line.

"What did you hear of my conversation with Dr. Barnes?"

The patient is a doctor? I'm not sure why that further piques my curiosity, but it does.

"Who?"

She opens the door to my room. "The patient in the room next to you. Did you hear what I was saying to him? It's important for HIPAA considerations. I'd need to report it if you heard his diagnosis."

Now, who's a lousy liar? "I didn't realize you were saying anything."

"Good," she says as she helps me back into bed. "That'll save me some paperwork. Everyone hates filling out forms."

"I know. Paperwork is the bane of my existence." I don't think I'll ever be able to develop a relationship with her, but it's worth a shot.

She eyes me suspiciously again. "Yes. Well, I'll send in your lunch shortly."

"Thank you." I favor her a "sweet as sugar" smile as she looks back over her shoulder before leaving my room.

I wait as long as possible to ensure she is not standing at my door. I dial Chase's number and roll my back to the door while cupping the phone, so my voice won't carry.

His phone goes to voicemail. I'm on my own.

Chapter 15

There must be some truth to this concussion diagnosis because my brain is working in slow motion. I have two fundamental issues at work here. First, I'm unclear about what is happening in the room behind me. I know what I thought I heard, and it certainly sounds like something nefarious. Still, that brings me to the second issue. I've never heard voices from a live person, and given the recent accident, this might all be some weird temporary cross-wiring of my brain.

I did go into the room by myself earlier, and there was not one glimmer of energy. Absolutely no voice like I heard several times through the headboard wall.

I should call the police.

No, that is an overreaction. What am I gonna say? I think I heard a comatose man telling me that his nurse was killing him.

Yeah, I don't think that tale is gonna fly. Even when *I* know there is something on the other side of the veil, I wouldn't consider my version of things credible if I were a juror at Peg's hypothetical arraignment trial.

I do have a feeling that the two, the nurse and the doctor, were in some sort of relationship. That would explain the anger and isolation feelings I lift from Peg when she grabs me. Her words and the emotions I feel running through her match up nicely to indicate an office romance gone badly. A relationship where one party was promised a future together. While the other decided the extramarital affair had become less exciting and required a lot of work like—well, a lot like being married, I suppose.

My lips curl, exposing my teeth. I absolutely despise cheaters. Dating is hard enough without having to contend with people that are "players." I'm not sure what, if anything, Peg is doing to compromise the good doctor's health, but maybe he deserves it.

Come on. You don't believe that, April.

Deep down in the wrath-filled crevices of my mind, a tiny, dark seed of female revenge resides. But in the civilized part—a more sizable portion of my brain, and the one wired correctly by my family—knows nobody should be physically harmed for an affair. Emotional scaring, public shaming, and emptying their bank accounts are fair game, but bodily harm is a no-no.

The doctor must be the unluckiest man in the world. What are the chances of having a cerebral hemorrhage and ending up with the woman you recently jilted as your primary caretaker? Yikes, if the doctor ever comes out of his coma, he might want to stay away from Vegas.

Women, too.

More importantly, and not to make this all about me, I hope Peg is no longer suspicious of me. I resolve to lay low until I'm released.

I try Chase's number again. My call goes to voicemail a second time.

If I genuinely believed in my skills, I would call the police with an anonymous tip. The problem is, I don't trust them. Their appearance is capricious, and often my readings of them are dubious at best.

Until, or unless, I become clear about what is going on in room 319, I'll keep to myself. It's not that I don't want to help; I'm just unsure if an actual crime is being committed.

I put my AirPods in and scroll my music service. My frustration has me channeling heavy metal. Typically, it's not my thing. It's Dusty's.

My sampling of Five Finger Death Punch, Of Mice and Men,

and more familiar old Metallica songs, reminds me why I'm not a headbanger.

"Can you still hear me?"

I close my eyes and hang my head. I hoped I wouldn't hear that now-familiar voice again. Shamefully, I don't answer him and hope he just goes away.

"I really need some help here. You're the only one who can save me."

Save him? Currently, I'm struggling to figure out how to save my sanity.

"I know you're there. I can feel you."

I draw an unsteady breath. If this is happening, if this isn't me stepping out of the bounds of sanity, I could be jeopardizing everything I've ever dreamed of being for someone I don't know. Still, I cannot ignore the man's cries. I relax and center myself.

"I'm here."

"Oh, thank you. I knew I felt you. My name is Andy."

"I'm April."

"April, I need your help," Andy says.

"I'm not sure I can. I don't even know how I hear you. Usually, I only hear folks that have already passed."

The long silence has me hoping that he has gone away or never reached out to me, and it was all a hallucination.

"Before too long, I won't be an exception to that rule. Peg is killing me."

His statement hits me like a gut punch. I'm convinced that I am honestly communicating with the man in room 319. With him so close to crossing the veil, it must be allowing us to share. Yet another unwelcomed paranormal surprise "gift."

Still, I don't believe him. *"Why would your nurse be trying to kill you?"*

"Because she hates me—and she is crazy."

"Why would your nurse hate you?"

His voice is barely audible in my head. *"Because I broke her heart. I told her I was planning on doing things I never intended to do."*

I'm right. As Granny always says, "He made his own bed; he can lie in it." Considering it is a life-and-death situation, I can't be that heartless. *"What do you need me to do?"*

"I need you to get me out of here."

I laugh out loud. *"You're hooked up to a bunch of machinery keeping you alive. Even if I had a car close by, I don't believe you would survive long enough to get wherever you want me to take you."*

"There must be some way. I must get home to my wife and kids. I need to explain to Evelyn what happened and apologize."

"Right. I suppose you're all prepared to come clean since you're on the edge of death. That is so classic male."

"Maybe. I'm not saying I deserve Evelyn's forgiveness. I'm only saying that I must apologize and beg for mercy."

I don't answer him as I consider what he said and the level of his sincerity.

"After all, we're all sinners. I'm sure even you have things in your life you're ashamed of and wish you could change."

I blow up my cheek and release the air in a frustrated manner. This is so not my problem. Yes, I understand the need to ask for forgiveness even when you know you might not receive it.

My best friend, Jackie Rains, and I had a falling out my senior year in high school. Jackie stole my boyfriend, Randy Leath, whom I had told we needed to take a break three weeks earlier.

After the blow-up, our mutual friends tried to convince me that Jackie didn't technically steal him from me since I had kicked Randy temporarily to the curb. Also, the fact that Randy asked Jackie out and not the other way around, by their take, made it more Randy's fault.

When Jackie had asked for my permission to go on a date with Randy, I told her exactly how I felt about her stealing my boyfriend. She told me I was crazy. I told her nobody needs a backstabber for a friend.

There are days I miss having Jackie as a friend. Besides, Randy isn't as cute as I remember him, and she probably did me a favor. It's challenging to contemplate being around her, given they are engaged.

Still, I wish I could go back and change that conversation some days. Perhaps soon, I'll even be compelled to apologize for how I behaved.

"Andy, when my brother comes back, we'll figure out a way to get you home to your family."

"Do you promise?"

My ears heat up as I wonder if I am overpromising. *"Yes."*

The door to my room opens, and I hold my breath, hoping to see Chase's handsome face walk through the door. I won't even scold him for disappearing on me.

"Lunch is served, Ms. Snow."

My hopes are dashed as Peg walks in carrying my tray. She has a smile on her face, and her attitude is much improved.

"Gotta go, Andy. It's Peg."

"The patients were supposed to be getting chicken and dumplings today for lunch." Peg grimaces and shakes her shoulders. "Trust me, that is only one step above pig slop."

She sets the tray in front of me, and my mouth starts to water.

"I thought you might prefer chicken fried steak, mashed potatoes, and green beans since you were hungry. I snuck this up from the physician assistant's cafeteria."

Bless her. This looks as good as Mama's cooking, and it smells divine. Even the green beans, which are not always my favorite, have bits of ham.

"Thank you," I gush.

"No worries. I have a couple of PA friends who trade favors with me."

It's amazing what a few conversations have done for our relationship. It's quite the one-eighty that Peg decided to go the extra mile to keep me happy.

"Now, you eat up. You need all your strength so that the doctor can release you."

There is an odd twitch on the left side of her face, and her smile fails to reach her eyes. My hand, grasped around the fork, pauses on the way to the promised land of mashed potatoes and gravy.

My phone rings as Peg leaves my room. It's Chase.

"Where are you?" I whine.

"I'm so sorry. The insurance adjuster called about the boat. I had to meet them at the marina to show them what is left of it. It took way longer than I expected."

"You could have at least called or texted me."

He grunts. "I know. I wanted to, but he wouldn't shut up. It's some serious cash, and the insurance company is trying everything possible to say it was negligence on my part."

"Negligence? It's like someone pulled that stupid log deliberately into our path. You were in the channel."

"I know, but his contention is that we should have been able to see it."

I take a bite of mashed potatoes and sigh. They are delicious.

"April? What are you doing?"

"Eating my lunch. At least the nurses here are looking out for me."

"Oh, please. Stop with the poor pretty princess."

I laugh at him as I cut a generous piece of cube steak. "Well, this princess has a favor to ask when you get here. You are on your way back to the hospital, right?"

"Since I'm already at the marina, I thought I might put in a couple hours and let Dusty come pick you up tonight when he gets in."

With the sudden change in Peg's attitude, I almost agree with Chase's plan. Still, I'll feel better once I'm out of here. If something seems out of kilter when I leave, I will try to get Andy out.

Maybe. I still feel like if I were to take Andy off his medical equipment, it would be the same as me killing him. I really don't want to be responsible for that.

"I know it's important, but if you can, I'd rather you come and see if you can get me discharged."

"Okay," he drawls. "Did something else happen?"

I don't want to tell him too much over the phone and have him turn into Captain America. "No. I just can't rest here, and I'm ready to go home."

He sighs. "Okay. I understand. Let me put a couple things right and lock up. I'll be there soon."

"Thank you, Chase."

I'm not sure if it is my relief from knowing my brother is coming to pick me up soon or the mega carb dose from my lunch, but as soon I hang up with Chase, I become incredibly sleepy.

I look longingly at the half-full lunch plate but put my fork down and lean back. I don't care to embarrass myself by falling asleep and face planting in my potatoes and gravy.

All the stress of the last few days is coming to a head, and I feel like I could sleep a week. My eyes close, and the last thing I remember is Andy hollering my name.

It's sunny, but there is a distinct chill in the air. I rotate my view and spot a grove of majestic oak trees to my left. The tips of their leaves are just now turning brown. The sky above is powder blue with white cotton ball patches speeding across, propelled by the wind.

The lawn chair I'm sitting on is cutting into the back of my thighs. I should have worn longer shorts, but these look cute. I have a game shirt on. It has the graphics of a red boar on a spit with a grinning elephant turning the crank over a blazing fire. The shirt reads *Bama Bar-B-Que*.

It's a tailgate party, and we must be playing Arkansas. I love game day.

Theresa and Susan sit across from me. Their mouths are going ninety to nothing, but all I hear is a loud continuous electronic tone. It sounds familiar. It is different than white noise, but I can't place it. Still, it agitates me.

I assume it's simply the scratchy seat irritating the back of my thighs.

Martin passes in front of me and hands me a beer. I unscrew the cap, and it falls between my feet. I watch the cap spin like a top between my uber-cute *Roll Tide* game day sandals that show off my crimson and white-striped pedicure.

My ankles are bound with multicolored nylon rope.

Something is cattywampus about this dream.

As I watch Stephen "Psycho Stevie" Nolin walk over to the table we have set up with a bounty of food, I'm clued in. I'm in a nightmare and not a pleasant tailgate memory. He steps back from the table, revealing the doe sprawled across the wooden surface. The doe stares at me with her large, dark eyes.

"To those that much is given, much is expected." The doe's black velvet lips mimic the words precisely while her body undulates with the mass of short, fat, white worms wriggling for a preferred position on her side.

I look from Susan to Martin, and they continue their conversation as if nothing about the situation is revolting. Psycho Stevie sits down next to me and bites into the sandwich in his hand. Maggots drop freely from between the sesame seed buns.

Man, I must have eaten something terrible to be having this sort of dream. This hasn't happened in years.

Everyone continues to talk, but their voices sound like one long electronic alarm. They laugh and joke but say nothing I can understand.

"April!"

Hearing an actual word in this crazy dream, more importantly my name, causes me to turn to the voice. An Arkansas fan stands over my chair. At least, I think he is an Arkansas fan. But his T-shirt has a picture of Porky Pig's face with "I'm a pig" written in red.

"April!"

What, dude? That's my name; don't wear it out. Nothing comes out of my mouth, just a long electronic alarm.

Weirdest dream ever.

"April, you have to get up now."

Pigman makes an excellent point. My legs must have a severe permanent indention from this stupid lawn chair.

"Wake up, April."

That sounds like a sage idea. Unfortunately, my dreams don't really work that way. They tend to release me when they want to.

I try to push Pigman out of the way. Just because he is handsome, with his chiseled jaw, aquiline nose, and shock of black hair, doesn't give him a free pass to get all up in my business.

He brings his hands down past my ears and presses his hands on my shoulders. The odd sensation of my sternum being crushed makes me grimace.

"You're in danger, April. It's Peg. She is coming for you!"

 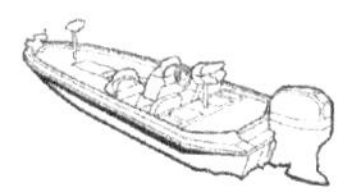

Chapter 16

My eyes pop open. Peg stands next to my IV, the loop with the injection port in her left hand and a syringe in her right. The surprise in her eyes tells me everything I need to know.

She hurries to stick the needle in the IV and misses as I yank it from my arm again, but I don't even feel it this time due to the adrenaline coursing through my body.

Seeing that I've foiled her plan, Peg pulls the syringe back and stabs at me with it. I grab her by the wrist and hold on for dear life as I struggle to clear the arm of the bed so I can be on my feet.

Her thoughts, desperate and murderous, flow through me. I can't know about Andy. No one must know. She doesn't want to, but she must kill me because I uncovered her plot, although it must be impossible for me to have discovered it.

I slide off the bed, half falling while continuing to battle, holding her wrist in one hand as I grab the front of her scrubs with the other. Peg throws a punch with her left. It's a hard but slow blow, and I tuck my chin so that her hand strikes the top of my forehead. A technique Chase has drilled into my head since I was a kid.

The nasty cracking noise of knuckles and fingers breaking is unmistakable. Peg screams out in pain.

I regain my footing and lower my right shoulder to catch her chest high as I use my strongest asset, my legs, to drive her backward. We strike the counter and bounce back. Suddenly, I fear that she will end up on top of me when we complete our fall to the tile floor. At the last moment, my foot plants firmly, and I drive her back into the countertop.

There is a rush of wind from her as the edge of the counter drives into her ribs. Her pain from the injuries she has already sustained emanates through me. Still, she is driven to finish her task at all costs.

Too late, I feel her ankle hook behind my leg, and in slow motion, I fall backward. I hold onto her wrist and bring her with me, afraid that she will inject me with whatever is in her hand if I release her.

My shoulder hits the tile floor first, and my head snaps back. White flashes of light fill my vision.

Peg's snarling mouth is inches from my face.

I flatten my thumb on my left fist as I hammer her rib. She grunts and tucks her arm to protect herself from another strike. I swing my fist again like a sledgehammer and catch her on the arm.

The desperation is building in her, and she focuses all the injustices of her entire life on me. I am what is the issue with her life.

I'm surprised when she leans forward and bites into my neck. Stupid me, I should have seen it coming. This isn't supposed to be a fair fight. It is supposed to be a fight to the death. She has already made her intentions perfectly clear.

I grab her ponytail and jerk it as viciously as possible without further consideration. She mews like an injured cat, and I continue to place as much weight as I can on my left arm to pull her to the side while keeping my right hand clamped around her wrist.

"Help! Help me!" Peg screams.

Her shouts embolden me, and I yank with all my might on her hair as I twist my body and roll. Like magic, I'm on top of her. I grab her right hand with both of mine and attempt to pry the syringe loose from her.

"What the heck is going on in here?" Benjamin steps in and feigns two attempts to break us up but looks confused about how to best accomplish the goal. "Help! I need some help in here."

I ignore Benjamin and continue to slam Peg's hand against the tile floor. Still, she holds onto the syringe with a death grip. She realizes that if she doesn't inject me in the next few seconds, her freedom is over.

Benjamin puts his arms around my waist and attempts to pick me up. I kick out with my right leg and catch him on the knee.

"Get the syringe from her!" I scream.

He hesitates.

I'm in this fight alone, but at least he quit trying to yank me off her.

A size thirteen laced shoe steps on Peg's wrist. I look up and see Benjamin glaring down at us.

"Let go of the syringe, Peg."

She stops struggling under me. Her hand opens, and I knock the syringe out of her grasp.

"She was complaining of pain, and when I went to give her some relief, she attacked me, Benny."

There is a rush of footsteps at the door, and I quickly glance over my shoulder. Two nurses—a female and a male—and a doctor have appeared.

"Benjamin, what's going on here?" The doctor, not much older than me, asks as he comes to Benjamin's side.

"I'm not really sure, Dr. Forrest."

"She is trying to poison me," I hiss as I push harder on Peg's shoulders.

"I was administering her medication, and she went crazy, Dr. Forrest."

"Let's start by getting off the floor," the doctor commands.

I don't like the idea of giving up my dominant position. Still, I can rationally understand that currently, it's my actions in doubt, not Peg's.

The syringe is a few feet from her, so I will have plenty

of warning if she goes for it. Plus, I can get behind the four professionals that work here for protection.

I push harder on her shoulders as I stand. As I take my hands off her, I backpedal until I am behind Benjamin and Dr. Forrest.

Peg stands and clutches her right hand. "She belongs in the mental ward, Dr. Forrest."

He looks at me, and I can tell Peg's words carry a lot of clout with him. "Ms. Snow, can I ask what triggered this?"

"She was trying to kill me to cover up that she is killing Andy in room 319."

Dr. Forrest's eyebrows come together. "Dr. Barnes?"

I shrug. "Andy." I point at Peg. "He was having an affair with her but wanted to come clean with his wife, Evelyn."

Dr. Forrest's expression sours, and he takes a step back from me. "How do you know this?"

"She is crazy, I tell you. She is making all this up," Peg interjects.

I give her the eye of death. "If you haven't noticed, these walls are pretty thin even with the headboards. Andy was asking me for help. I was only waiting on my brother to get here."

The fact it isn't a complete lie helps with my delivery. Dr. Forrest appears to relax as he contemplates what I say.

He turns to Benjamin and points at Peg. "Is she the one he was seeing?"

Benjamin shakes his head. "I didn't know Dr. Barnes like that."

The doctor's nose wrinkles as he questions Peg. "How did you get assigned to care for someone you were involved with?"

Peg rolls her eyes. "It's not like anybody knew. That is why they're called secret affairs."

"So, you're responsible?"

Peg appears aghast. "No. I simply want to help the man I love." She points at me. "But then this crazy one attacked me. What are you going to do with her?"

"I'd say you're not going to do a darn thing with her. That crazy one belongs to me."

I nearly cry when I hear Chase's voice. Finally, the cavalry has arrived. It is not necessary now, but it's always good to have help.

"It's not that easy." Peg points her finger at me. "I'm charging her with assault."

"That's rich," I scoff. "It's you who is assaulting Andy and me. Wait till he wakes up. He'll tell everyone."

Peg smirks at me.

"What?" I turn and look at Dr. Forrest and Benjamin.

The female nurse behind us speaks up. "Dr. Barnes coded a few minutes ago. That is why we were all so close."

"Coded?" I ask.

Dr. Forrest runs his hands through his hair. "He has passed, Ms. Snow."

The news knocks the breath out of me. Combined with the fading adrenaline, I can't catch my wind and feel faint.

I was supposed to help Andy. I had promised to save him by getting him out of here. Instead, the tables were turned, and he came to me and saved me. I stab my finger in Peg's direction. "She did that. She killed him in cold blood. She was angry because he was breaking off the relationship."

"That is ridiculous. Andy and I were soulmates. As soon as I nursed him back to health, he planned to leave that wife of his and marry me."

"What is in the syringe, Peg?" Dr. Forrest asks.

She glares at the doctor. "I already told you, something for her pain."

"Humor me. What is it?"

"Toradol."

Dr. Forrest tilts his head. "You sure about that?"

"What sort of question is that?"

"A sincere one," he says.

"What is tore it all?" Chase asks.

"Toradol. Basically, injectable ibuprofen," I answer.

"Really?" Chase steps forward. "I'll make you a promise, Peg. If you inject yourself with that souped-up aspirin, I'll commit my sister to a health clinic."

"Chase!" I punch him on the arm.

He shoots me a sideways grin. "It's a square deal."

Peg looks at the syringe over her shoulder. She doesn't move.

"It's not Toradol, is it, Peg?"

She bites her lower lip and looks away from Dr. Forrest.

"It is insulin, isn't it," he continues to push her.

She turns back to him. Her eyes are wide and wild. "Look at you, Doctor. Aren't you oh-so smart now? Y'all are all alike. Pompous blowhards who think you're better than the rest of us. I thought Andy was different." She crosses her arms across her chest as tears stream down her face. "He promised me!"

Dr. Forrest, to his credit, is unphased by her outburst. As for me, I slink further behind Benjamin, Chase, and the doctor. I've already gone one tough round with Peg, and I don't care to go in the ring for a second.

Dr. Forrest holds out his hand to her. "Come on, Peg. Come down to security with me, and we'll sort this out."

"And if I don't?" She raises her chin.

"Then I guess we'll have to hogtie you and drag you out of here. I'd hate that. You're much more of a professional than that."

Her shoulders slump.

Forrest moves closer to her, his hand still extended.

"It's not my fault," Peg cries.

"Nobody is judging you, Peg. Take a walk with me. Okay?"

She accepts his hand and takes a shaky breath. She follows Dr. Forrest's lead out the door with her eyes on the floor. The two nurses other than Benjamin follow the doctor cautiously.

When they are out of sight, I turn my attention to Benjamin. He has a hand over his mouth, staring up at the ceiling as if praying.

"Well, that was a little intense," Chase says cheerfully.

"Lord, I should get combat pay today." Benjamin shakes his head.

"I want to go home."

Benjamin flinches. "Yes. Right. Give me a moment to get the discharge papers together."

He steps wide around me as he makes his way out of the room.

Chase raises his eyebrows as he gives me one of his patented goofy grins. "Making friends everywhere you go, Tink."

"Can it."

"Hey." He points at my chest. "I told you it did that."

I look down at my hospital gown. A bright violet light emanates through the thin fabric.

My hand comes up and clutches the amulet to my chest. The magical jewelry piece my Granny left with earlier today.

 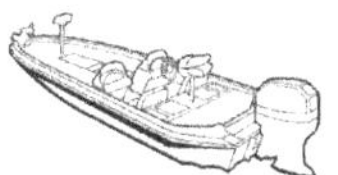

Chapter 17

I can't stop shaking, and I keep playing the dangerous "what if" game in my mind. It's a coin toss if I'll break into a chest-heaving sob or attempt to link a lengthy line of random obscenities together and scream them at the truck windshield. Actual cuss words, not the Mama-approved versions.

Chase may not be psychic, but he can read his sister. He hasn't said a word since I got in the pickup truck with him.

It's his stupid fault. If it hadn't been for his cockamamie fishing tournament, none of this would have happened to me.

It's always easy to deconstruct things after the fact. Still, as I examine it, I believe I self-sabotaged my birthday because I didn't want to come home until I was settled in Atlanta.

If Chase hadn't called me for a favor, my first time back home would have been the Fourth of July. I would have been in Atlanta for a month, most likely paranormal-free.

I glare at the white pillowcase on the dash. It conceals the new bane of my existence. The amulet that miraculously reappeared around my neck.

That is apropos. The glowing gem is like an albatross around my neck.

Alright. That is admittedly a bit dramatic since it's not on my neck right now. Still, that is where it longs to be. I can feel it calling to me.

I can't even fabricate a far-fetched explanation for its appearance this time. The theory the boat accident ejected me so forcibly that my wrist shoved through a necklace is a tough sell. Explaining how it escaped Granny's pocket and reappeared around my neck is impossible to ignore as anything but magic.

The level of paranormal activity I have experienced in the last seventy-two hours is nearly unprecedented. Before Nana taught me how to defend against the voices, they were a constant intrusion in my life.

I had forgotten how disconcerting it is to constantly see and hear things other people can't.

What really bites is all I can focus on is holding the necklace that has claimed me. Chase suggested we put it in the pillowcase so I wouldn't be tempted. Even fully concealed, it has more attraction than a double icing cupcake, and I could really use a cupcake right now.

What I wouldn't give to be Chase. He is the only person in our family who flat-out rejects the existence of anything supernatural. My life would be so much easier if I won that Snow DNA lottery. Instead, I hit the Powerball for weirdness.

I can't even feel sufficiently sorry for myself without feeling guilty. I made Andy a promise. An ill-advised promise I never could have kept due to his condition. Despite my failure to help him, he hung around on this side of the veil long enough to save my life.

Peg, a woman I barely know, really tried to kill me. Just considering it makes me feel vulnerable.

If Andy had not woken me up, or if it had taken him five seconds longer, I wouldn't have known she spiked my IV with insulin. I would have just crashed and then passed like Andy.

The awakening of my "gifts," my inability to save Andy's life, and the brush with death has me teetering at the edge of an abyss of deep despair. I don't know if I can work through these issues.

I was raised to be grateful and look at the positives in life. Bless it. Lord knows I've had tremendous opportunities and, more importantly, capitalized on them. Plus, I'm so near my big payoff.

But today, it all feels at risk of imploding. Today, I'm the world's biggest loser, and in all probability, I should be dead right now except for the kindness of a deceased stranger.

It's a lot to wrap my mind around. I'm not doing as good of a job with it as I would hope.

"Chase, can you put that in the glove compartment for me?" I point at the dash.

He cuts his eyes to me. "The pillowcase?"

"Yes, please."

He leans over and stows the amulet in the glove compartment with his right hand. "Better?"

Not until it's been in there long enough for me to forget about it. "Yeah, thank you."

Chase sighs lightly as he taps the side of the steering wheel with no rhythm. He is agitated about something.

"I'm not sure if this is the right time to tell you, but since you helped, I figure you'd want to know. The police department called off the search for Jaxx."

Like one too many Jenga blocks pulled from the stack, I teeter on the edge of the dark chasm of depression. Standing at the cliff, I am about to lose my mind, and my brother accidentally bumps me in the back.

His timing is impeccably bad.

"Did you hear me, April?"

"Yes," I croak.

"The National Guard loaned the police two helicopters and crews yesterday. They searched for over eight hours. They didn't find any sign of Jaxx—they did find a pot field out by the Talbot farm."

My ire bubbles over at his insensitivity. "What, that makes it a success?"

"Well, no. But at least something came of it."

I wave my hand at him and scoot closer to the door as I press my forehead to the side window. "Just don't, Chase. I can't right now."

"Geez, why are you being this way?"

I need to let it go. It's just Chase being Chase. He doesn't mean anything by it.

Still, I can't let it go and turn on him. "For Pete's sake, Chase. You told me a little boy is assumed dead by the authorities. The son of a friend of mine who was murdered the other day. Do you expect me to be happy about the guard finding pot plants?"

He remains silent, and I immediately regret losing my temper. Blowing up on Chase is what I would imagine it would be like to kick a cocker spaniel puppy.

"I apologize. I didn't consider the tremendous stress you must be under with your assignment."

My nose wrinkles as I try to discern Chase's screwball syntax. "Assignment?"

The headlights of a passing car light the whites of his eyes. "Yes. I assume by your behavior, you were assigned to keep Gemma, Jaxx, and the dead doctor safe. I just didn't know."

I'm holding my redneck in by the hair, but I'm losing my grip on her. "You're not funny, Chase. You need to be quiet."

He scoffs. "You're going to bow up and act tough with me?"

I readjust my seat. "What does that mean?"

"Just saying it looked like you had your fill of fighting Peg today. I saw you hiding behind the rest of us. I have to say I was quite surprised."

"She bit me!" I yell.

"And what?"

"She was fighting dirty!"

Chase laughs uncontrollably.

"Quit laughing."

"She tried to kill you. Did you really expect a fair fight?" he asks.

"I really, really don't like you right now." I turn toward my window and watch the shadows of pines pass.

"Do you want me to go through a drive-thru?"

"I'm not talking to you." My treasonous stomach growls.

"I'll take that as a yes," he says with too much glee for my liking.

Chase attempts to make up for his rudeness by bribing me with a bucket of Kentucky Fried Chicken. It's a good bribe, but I'm in no mood to let him out of the doghouse yet.

My stomach grumbles all the way to my parents' driveway.

I spot Dusty's black GTO as we pull up the drive. "I thought Dusty was coming in late tonight," I say.

"He sent me a text before your brawl telling me he was able to take the three o'clock flight into Huntsville since he finished his meetings early."

Dusty being home irritates me all over again. I love him, but he is obsessed with my paranormal abilities. Chase will readily accept I had a "hunch" about Peg being a killer. Dusty will assume I used my "gifts" to uncover her plan.

Talking is not on my list of “want to do” things. If I have my druthers, I will eat way too much fried chicken, curl up for a short carb-induced coma, and leave for Tuscaloosa when my eyes open tomorrow.

Chase opens the glove compartment and pulls out the pillowcase. He makes to hand it to me.

"I'm carrying the chicken," I say as I step down out of his truck.

As we walk up the stairs to the back porch, the sliding glass door opens. "They can rebuild her. They have the technology. We can make her better than she was..." Dusty says as he braces his arms in the entryway.

"Bite me," I say as I duck under his arm.

"Welcome home to you, too," Dusty says at my back. "Is that fried chicken?"

"No. The Colonel has branched out into pizza, and they put it in a bucket, too." I flop onto one of the kitchen stools.

"How..." Dusty stutters.

"Yes, it's chicken," I say.

"What's with her?" Dusty asks Chase.

"She got her butt kicked, and she is sore about it," Chase says.

I slam a chicken breast down on my paper plate, and breading flies off the plate onto the floor. "I did not lose that fight."

"Well, you didn't exactly win it." Chase tosses the pillowcase next to my plate.

The power from the amulet tickles my hand closest to it. I push it away from me, and it emits a light glow.

"What is in the bag," Dusty asks.

"Some weird necklace that glows in the dark," Chase says.

Dusty grabs for it, and at first, I almost snatch it back. Still, I really don't care to touch it again.

He shakes it out of the pillowcase and whistles. "That is one humungous rock. Is that a ruby?"

"Blood amethyst," I say, and take a bite of chicken.

"I'm not usually into jewelry, but I really like this piece for some reason."

Looking up from my piece of chicken, I notice the dreamy look in Dusty's eyes. "It's cursed. I'd put it back before you start obsessing over it."

Dusty gives a nervous chuckle. "Seriously?"

"I'm no expert, but I don't think anything good will come from that piece of jewelry."

"Where did it come from?" Dusty asks.

"It got stuck on April's arm when we crashed the boat," Chase says as he opens the fridge.

"First off, we didn't crash the boat. You crashed the boat. Second, you know there is no way I happened to come out of the water with a necklace around my arm, Chase."

He twists the cap off a beer. "There's no other explanation for it."

"Right. Hand me one of those, please," I say.

Chase hands me a beer. He walks out of the kitchen, leaving Dusty looming over me.

"Are you going to eat the thighs?" he asks.

"No." I fish two of them out of the bucket and hand them to him as he grabs a paper towel.

"Thanks," Dusty says as he follows Chase out of the kitchen.

I'm shocked that Dusty didn't stay and press me with more questions about today. I suppose it proves just how lousy my company is tonight.

It's to be expected. My entire world has been turned upside down the last few days. Even if it wasn't for the paranormal activity, I would be at the edge of my sanity. Throw in the supernatural events, and it's a wonder I'm not sitting in a corner drooling right now.

Truthfully I'm not sure how far off I am from that. This whole trip has me unhinged, and I'm not even confident that returning to Tuscaloosa will put things back for me.

I stare down at the amulet Dusty left outside of the pillowcase. The desire to touch it is genuine.

I sigh lightly as my resolve falls. I stick a greasy hand out and lay it on the stone. Immediately it glows a bright violet that lights the room like some weird disco ball from a Prince concert in 1984.

Continuing to stare at it, I remove my hand and open my beer. One long drag and half the bottle is empty. No, I don't think it'll make the situation better, but perhaps if I drink enough, it won't be the first thing on my mind.

I've come too far and worked too hard to have everything come undone here at the finish line. I must set this right.

Besides, what good are my paranormal “gifts”? Can they save a little boy's life? No. Can I help people who have reached out to me? No. So why deal with them?

There is not one good reason that I can think of.

I take another long draw on my beer, nearly emptying it.

Squinting, I weigh my options. Granny said that she would put the amulet up in her collection. Somehow, it decided it didn't want to go and found its way back to me.

My paranormal powers were almost nonexistent before I encountered the amulet. I'm convinced that it is the reason I'm experiencing the sudden rush of supernatural events.

I walk over to the fridge and pull out another beer. Twisting the cap off, I lean against the refrigerator and eye the amulet as if it will fly across the room and hook around my neck again.

There is no choice. I can't put my entire life at risk over this piece of jewelry. I must get rid of it. In my mind, there is only one place for it to go.

Gingerly, I lift the serpentine chain into the pillowcase and flip the amulet in with one finger. Swinging the pillowcase in my right hand while holding my fresh beer in the left, I exit through the sliding glass door and make my way down the porch toward the dock.

It's as if the jewelry has a life of its own. I feel it tugging at my senses, begging me not to dispose of it.

My resolve is firm. I have no use for this in my life. I didn't ask for it, and I don't need it.

Still, when I make it to the dock, I hesitate. My attraction to the piece is a growing addiction.

I sit down on the edge of the dock, laying the pillowcase beside me, and pull off my tennis shoes. I can just trail my toes in the murky water below.

Why does everything have to be so complicated for me?

It's not really about me. I'm sad that three people I know have died in two days. Something about being around that much death pushes me toward the dark side.

These events have even knocked the shine off of my upcoming graduation and employment at Master, Lloyd, and Johnson. It's like the joy of life has disappeared. In its place is this purple piece of jewelry that mocks me.

A stupid cursed necklace from a dead woman. A woman who killed herself. Is that it? Is that why I'm feeling so down right now? Is there something about the amulet that makes life seem hopeless?

Yes. It must be. I can't think of another time I've ever felt so distraught. It must be the amulet.

I push up to my feet and shove my hand into the pillowcase. The stone shines brighter than ever, nearly blinding me with the purple light as my hand heats up. I can feel it drinking in the passion I feel. It knows what is coming and rails against it with all its magic.

My hand goes behind my head, and I whip my arm down and to the side. I throw the amulet as far as I can and listen to the pleasing plunk as it penetrates the lake's surface.

"You can have it back, Dionis. I don't want it."

I sit on the dock and finish my beer with a grin. Now I'm free of that demanding stone.

The sun touches the horizon on the lake, casting odd shadows from the trees. The temperature drops, and I wrap my arms around myself.

The euphoria of ridding myself of the magical item subsides. The sadness creeps back into my spirit, and I can't seem to leave the dock.

There are footsteps behind me. There is a slight shuffle to them, informing me it is Dusty.

He pulls his shoes off and sits next to me. He hands me another beer. I think to tell him no thank you but decide I'm on a roll, so why stop now.

"Tough day?" he asks.

"Understatement of the year," I grumble.

"This too shall pass," he says.

"I wish I could be sure."

"Chase is pretty torn up that you're upset with him."

I wrinkle my forehead as I glare at him. "He is tore up? He was insensitive about the fact Jaxx is probably dead."

Dusty's eyebrows rise as his eyes open wider. "How do you figure that, April?"

"Because he was more interested in the fact that the helicopters found a pot field."

Dusty shakes his head. "Come on now. You know Chase better than that. He doesn't do well with losing, and he is terribly upset about that little boy. That is one of the reasons why I cut my meeting short to come home. First, I was worried about you being in the hospital, and second I could tell he really needed somebody to talk to. That boy hates to lose, and that is how he views what happened to Jaxx. You know him. He is a helper."

Dusty is correct, and the shame of thinking such ill thoughts about my brother compounds with all the other sad feelings I have, and they overwhelm me. I hiccup a couple of sobs, and tears well in my eyes.

"Hey, now. There's no crying at the lake house." Dusty tries to make light of the situation.

I'm at serious risk of blowing a snot bubble, and I don't have any Kleenex. I manage to stop the stupid sob hiccupping, but the tears flow in earnest.

Dusty puts his arm around me and pulls me toward him. I don't resist. Instead, I put my head against his shoulder."

"I promise you it will get better, Tink," he says.

Looking up, I lock eyes with him. "No, it's not. I feel it. It's going to get worse."

 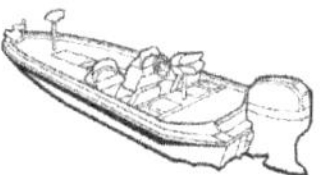

Chapter 18

With Dusty's help, I shake the blues off sufficiently to make my way inside the lake house, take a shower, and get ready for bed. But now I'm staring at the stupid picture of dogs playing poker I made my daddy buy me when I was little. I should have thrown that old, framed poster away years ago. Still, since I'm never moving home, it'll be Mama's issue now.

Reaching over, I turn off the lamp. The room transforms into pitch dark, and the recent encounter with the ghost of Dionis sends a prickle of fright across my chest. I grab my phone, more for the light than the distraction of anything I might read.

This is all so silly. I've simply allowed myself to get sucked back into my family's craziness. This isn't my life anymore, and I don't have to concern myself with it. I am April May Snow. I'm destined to become the preferred defense counsel to all well-heeled clients in the Southeast and the woman all future law students will aspire to emulate. High-powered clientele will seek my services.

I'm not some freak with a redneck streak from a small town on a lake in North Alabama, or some crazy lady who hears voices and sees ghosts. No. That is not me, and I reject those definitions.

There is no such thing as fate in life. If there were, free will would be an oxymoron.

I scroll to the Steve Madden site and cruise through the uber-cool sandal section. I can't wait until I have an unlimited budget for shoes. Shoes and cupcakes are the best, but shoes edge out for the win by a nose. Because having extra money to buy more shoes doesn't affect my weight. Cupcakes—that is a different story.

I feel better now that I've centered myself and remember that tomorrow I will leave all this behind for the last time. All this paranormal and small-town craziness—it's no longer my monkey. I'll leave it for other people. I've got bigger plans for my life.

Worn smooth by this trip's events, I snuggle into my pillows and wait for sleep. I'm plenty tired, understandably. Still, my brain continues to churn too much.

The thought crosses my mind to check in with Martin and get the gory details on his "meet the parents" horror date trip. As I find his contact information, I notice it is already eleven, which is midnight in DC.

There is no need to get Penny's insecurities stirred up by calling him at midnight. Them being at her parents wouldn't be helpful, either.

What has that goofball gotten into? Penny is the first girl he has hooked up with during the two years we've been best friends. In some ways, his new relationship has thrown me for a loop. It was a long-standing joke that neither of us had dated in years. I always assumed that neither of us would bother with that distraction until we were settled in our law careers.

And Penny? I mean, she is not unattractive. I suppose she could be considered beautiful if you like petite girls with ample bosoms and luxurious, chestnut hair. Still, with the constant flashing of her perfect white teeth and her "OMG" expression, she is *so* not Martin's type.

He is such a good friend, I only hope he knows what he is doing. I want the best for him. Besides, I would hate to be forced to mess Penny's perfect teeth up with my fist if she were to crush his heart.

The sun warms my face, and I feel my lips stretch into a smile. I adjust my view from the bright-blue sky, and Martin laughs at my side.

I pan the view and realize we're on a blanket at the Quad under one of the oak trees. Denny Chimes sounds off to my right, raising chill bumps on my neck.

This is one of our favorite places. How many times have we brought a bagged lunch to the Quad, sat, and people watched?

Since I've been at the university for so long, there are very few things I'll miss. Football games—because who doesn't like winning national championships? —and hanging out with Martin at the Quad. Those two things I know I will miss.

A feminine laugh that reminds me of a hyena with a stray chicken bone stuck in its throat cackles in from my side, and I cringe. Swiveling to my left, I'm horrified to see Penny next to Martin.

She is not supposed to be here. We never invite dates to our friend times. This is Martin's and my thing.

Penny continues to laugh or choke, I'm not sure which, as the resentment builds in me. I have the odd urge to pop her in the mouth.

Relax. I'm not gonna do it. I have *some* self-control.

Still, why is she here? Surely Martin wouldn't have invited her to come to our place. That would not be cool. I bet she found out somehow and insisted. That sounds more probable. With her misconceptions about Martin's and my relationship, she blackmailed him into allowing her to tag along.

Wake up, Martin. This is the rest of your life staring you down.

Penny finally stops with the weird laughing, but only long enough to suck in a breath. Before Martin or I can speak, she somehow segues into a pointless story about people I don't know and some drama they are involved in. I truly am amazed at how long the girl can talk without breathing. It shouldn't be physically possible. She would make a fantastic pearl diver.

I'm about to interrupt her, not to say anything of any merit, just simply because I can't stand to listen to her talk any longer. Like a summoned angel, a pizza delivery girl appears out of thin air and distracts me with two pizzas.

Martin pays the girl in cash.

I now realize this is a dream. Martin and I always split the tab, and he is typically broke, leaving me to cover the tip portion of the bill.

"Thanks for the treat, Martin," I say.

"Anything for my two girls."

I frown while I rerun Martin's statement through my mind. His girls?

Maybe the strain of having Penny and me together is causing him to say bizarre stuff. It does have to be stressful. I recognize we are one misspoken word away from a colossal drama atom bomb, and Martin will be the one to suffer the brunt of its destruction.

He would deserve it. Why did he invite Penny to our place?

Because he is a softhearted bonehead. If Martin wanted to bring Penny here by themselves without my knowledge, that would have been a—look at me ... I'm trying to apply logic to a ridiculous dream. Who says Martin would even do something this foolish? He's not the most socially adept, but he is not an ignoramus.

Which begs the question, if it's my dream, what if I *do* pop Penny in the mouth? It's not like the dream police will throw me in jail. Even if they did, I have a get out of jail free card called waking up.

I giggle as the thought takes root in my mind. I watch Penny's mouth open and close at a frightening pace as she plops a grease-dribbling slice of extra-pepperoni pizza on her paper plate. If I time this perfectly, I might be able to pop her in the face when she is taking a bite of her pizza.

That would be a riot.

Dad-burnit. The temperature suddenly drops like forty

degrees. I know the spring breezes can still blow cold in Alabama, but it felt like early summer ten seconds ago. I cover my chest with my arms and try to conserve some heat. Still, I shake uncontrollably against the frigid blast.

Studying Martin and Penny as they eat their pizza, they don't seem bothered by the sudden drop in temperature. Penny, I understand. The girl is generating enough heat by the motion of her lips to keep her warm. But Martin, with his casual, attentive boyfriend nodding of the head, isn't working up any warmth.

Something is cockamamie about this dream. More so than my usual dreams. This one has taken a turn for the worst and seems to be channeling the nightmare from the hospital. I want out.

Another chill racks my body. It is so aggravating when I want to wake from a bad dream, and it refuses to cut me loose. Even sans the preternatural frosty breeze, watching Martin direct his dreamy eyes lovingly toward Penny has transformed this into my personal voyeuristic purgatory.

Any more of this sappy romance book date scene, and I'll want to bop him in the face, too.

I holler in pain as something bizarre happens to my left shoulder. It's as if a cold burn is ripping through it.

My eyes pop open. I gasp, and my breath catches so hard at the back of my throat that it feels like I tore my esophagus.

Dionis leans over me. Her hand rests on my shoulder.

My body constricts, and my ribs flare with pain as I attempt to scream. Dionis is not the hauntingly beautiful translucent blue from her last visit. Swollen with a greenish-gray tint, her flesh hangs loosely from her bones in mottled, decaying jagged strips. Her shredded, patterned sundress drips with black fetid mud.

It's not a good look for her.

I think to duck and roll off the edge of the bed like I did the last time she visited my room. Instead, I have an unexpected moment of clarity. Dionis will not leave until I help her with what caused her to be called to me. So, I'll have to put my fear aside and establish what she needs me to accomplish.

Besides, I'm not going to be able to outrun her if she doesn't want me to.

Quickly, I pray for courage. Lord knows I don't have the latent courage required to deal with the decaying visage before me.

I suck in a breath and center my emotions. "What do you want, Dionis?"

She points a long bony finger at me. I nearly wet the bed.

In one millisecond, I just spent all the courage I prayed for. I don't know why Dionis wants me or what she plans to do with me once she has me, but I am thoroughly wigged out now. To make matters worse, where I could have fled my room earlier and sought comfort in one of my brothers' rooms, now I am frozen with fear. Perfect.

Dionis crooks her finger, motioning for me to follow her.

Nope. I've seen this in at least a hundred ghost movies. I am not following the half-decayed ghost anywhere. I don't care how much Granny may have liked this lady when she was alive. I've learned that being on the other side of the veil changes people's personalities.

Dionis tilts her head at an unusually steep angle, forcing me to tense again. She makes threatening "mom eyes" at me, and I never thought anyone could top my mama's glare of death. Her expression shakes me, but I firmly hold my ground—I only hope she doesn't flash three-inch fangs— because then I'm tearing a hole through the drywall in my room to escape.

"Sorry. I can't go with you." I try to reason with her.

She makes a beckoning motion with her right hand. I can sense the agitation building in the air.

"I wish I could, Dionis. But I have to get up early tomorrow."

She halts her motion through my closed door and floats back toward my bed. I pull my sheets up around my neck as if they are made of special ghost Kevlar.

The room fills with a purple light, and Dionis pulls the amulet from under her shift. Deliberately she removes the chain from around her neck and holds out the jewelry toward me.

I'm now embarrassed that I threw the amulet in the lake. Honestly, I thought it would be Granny asking me if I had seen the jewelry, and I would eventually crack and tell her what I did. I had no idea that it would be a ghost bringing me back the piece that I disposed of.

Dionis shakes the amulet in my face. Obviously, I have waited too long to accept it from her.

"No, you keep it. It's yours," I say lamely.

Again, she sends me that expression conveying I have said something incredibly disrespectful.

That is okay. I've had years of practice ignoring the deadly mom stare. True, this is the first time I've received it from a decaying corpse, but my mama can make anybody's blood run cold with only a look. Dionis will have to try something much scarier to get me to obey.

She beckons me toward the door again. "Come with me now."

The voice, her voice, sends a chill down my spine. It sounds as if it gurgles up from the depth of the lake. It has an inexplicable ancient sound to it. It leaves me wondering if it is Dionis's voice or if she is the mouthpiece for something else I desperately need to avoid.

Either way, I notice the increasing tension in the energy field. The last thing I care to do is frustrate a ghost to the point that they go rogue.

"Give me a second," I say as I put my feet on the floor.

In answer, Dionis floats to the door and waits patiently as I slip my tennis shoes on.

I could scream right now, and my brothers would come to the rescue. The thing is, I don't know what Dionis's powers are, nor her intent at this point. As much as I'd like to have some help, I have no desire to pull my brothers into an ambush.

Reluctantly, I walk to my door and open it to follow Dionis as she floats through our home.

As I follow her, I promise myself I will refuse to get too close to the lake or walk out onto the dock. I'd be lying if I said I don't have a niggling idea that Dionis plans to drown me in the lake for me attempting to destroy the amulet.

She floats through the kitchen wall out onto the deck. I pull open the sliding door as quietly as possible. I'm still not ready to pull my brothers into this situation until I know what is happening.

I'm relieved when Dionis takes a right off the back porch toward the driveway. But I'm perplexed as she floats next to Chase's pickup truck.

I stand at the front bumper of his truck, she by the driver's door. She points toward the vehicle, and her hand goes through the driver's window.

"Yes. Truck," I say dumbly as I wait for Dionis to explain herself. In frustration, I add, "There is no way Chase will let me drive the truck if that is your idea. We can take my car."

Dionis jabs her mottled gray finger through the driver's window several times in a hostile manner. The breeze intensifies as her energy leaves little doubt in my mind that she is losing patience with me.

"I'm sorry, but I don't have the keys, Dionis."

She stretches her neck at another impossible angle and points at the truck again. All four doors unlock simultaneously.

I clench my jaw, and my teeth clack together rudely.

Our trash cans blow over from the increasing wind she has stirred, causing me to flinch.

I think best under pressure. I am under tremendous stress, and an epiphany pops out of my addled brain like a magical diamond egg.

Dionis wants me to look in the truck.

Peaches. Why the extended version of charades when I know she has a gurgling—albeit disconcerting—voice available?

"Okay," I say. "I just didn't understand you."

I'll look in the truck to appease her. So help me, if there is another piece of cursed jewelry in it, I'm going to be majorly ticked off.

I check the driver's door first. Nothing under the seat or on the dash. I find a pouch of Red Man tucked in between Chase's seat and the console. That's a big no-no. I can use that as blackmail information with Mama.

Then again, Chase would make up some explanation about keeping it to draw out the poison from bee stings. Mama would buy his Boy Scout “be prepared” story, too. She always believes Chase.

I huff and sit up in the seat. Craning my neck, I look in the passenger floorboard. Immaculately clean. That is one thing about Chase, he keeps his toys in pristine condition.

Deciding Dionis will not leave me alone until I find whatever she thinks I should be seeing, I resolve to check the rest of the truck.

I slide down out of the truck and open the back door. Leaning in, I check under the seats. All clear under the driver's seat. I swivel my head and jerk away, striking my head against the back of the driver's seat.

Laughing, I try to calm my heart as I reach in for the furry little devil under the back bench seat. "Well, how did you get lost under there, little buddy?"

The beating of my heart slows as sadness waves over me, and tears well in my eyes. My nose tingles, and I wonder why Dionis would torment me by reminding me about Jaxx's death.

Only one thing comes to mind. Dionis knows I am close to the pit of despair. She aims to pull me in like the amulet pulled her to her death. How it coaxed her into the darkness, convincing her that life was no longer worth living.

Grandpa Snow always said, "Misery enjoys company, and the most miserable require the most company."

Nope. That's not me. Chase had a crass manner of explaining it to me, but none of this has been my fault. Not Gemma, Andy, and certainly not Jaxx, whom I have never even met.

It is a sad state of affairs; this is true. But this is not my life.

I extend my arm to tuck Jaxx's Winnie-the-Pooh bear back under the bench seat where I found him.

A familiar weight falls around my neck, and something hard slaps against my sternum. As a vision runs across my mind, a rush of energy flows through me.

I want to scream, but nothing comes out when my mouth

drops open.

Chapter 19

"Leonard, what are we gonna do?"

"For the last time, shut your mouth, Chester."

"But you stabbed her. Why did you do that?"

"No. Don't you blame this on me. I told you to tie her up. A simple task, and once again, as always, you failed to carry out your end of the bargain."

"You saw her. She went crazy on me."

"And you outweigh her by fifty pounds. Do your job, Chester. That is all I ever ask of you is to do your job. Do you? No. I constantly must clean up after you. Now, this whole deal has gone south. And it's your fault."

The room jostles, and my eyes open. All I see is the color navy. The air is scarce and heavy with the scent of cigarette smoke. I breathe faster as I try to pull in more air.

"You really screwed the pooch this time, Chester. It won't surprise me if Nolin backs out of this deal."

"No, he won't. He wanted the kid, and we got him for him."

"Think it through. If Stephen has his kid, the police will think he killed his wife."

"Well, that helps us. Doesn't it?"

"How stupid are you? You really believe he is gonna pay us so he can go to jail for murdering his wife?"

"Oh."

"Right. Oh."

I've run out of air and am hyperventilating. "I can't breathe," I whine. The voice is not my own.

"Shut your mouth, kid."

The man's command only intensifies the anxiety I feel. The pace of my panting increases.

"I swear I don't see how this can get any worse. Chester, check on that kid. Make sure he doesn't suffocate. I told you not to put the blanket around his head so tight."

"You said to make sure he couldn't identify us, Leonard," Chester grumbles.

"Just do it!"

I flinch from the sudden light blinding my sight but greedily suck in the fresh air. My eyes adjust to the sunlight, and I stare up at the bushy, blond mustache of a man.

"Better, little guy?"

I look up from his bushy mustache, past his bulbous, red nose, and into his crystal-blue eyes. Something is wrong. Something is terribly wrong. "I want my mommy," I cry.

"And I want a beachside condo in Panama City. I guess we're both out of luck, little man."

"Chester, I said make sure he could breathe. Not chat him up."

The man with the mustache makes an odd face at me as he acts like he is repeating the other man's words. Then he disappears from my view.

The room we are in shakes again. I try to move my legs, but my feet stay together. I can't roll over because my hands are together behind my back.

I'm so scared, and I don't want to be here. I don't understand.

The movement of the room stops. I hear doors. Chilly air rushes in, and even though I want to be brave, it makes me cry. My warm tears stream down my face and collect on my lip. I taste the salt creeping into my mouth.

"What are we gonna do with him, Leonard?"

"The plan remains the same."

"But you said..."

"I said his dad might not pay us. If he doesn't, we don't tell him where to find the boy. If he comes through with his side of the deal and decides he wants his kid, he can pay us and do whatever he wants to do. But our plan doesn't change."

A door opens, and I'm pulled up into a sitting position. I'm in the back of a car, not a room like I thought. Not my mom's or my aunt's car. I've never been in this one before.

A man with dark black hair and eyes like the other man's looks at me. "Hi, Jack. Are you ready to go for a hike?"

"I think his name is Jaxx with the letter x."

The dark-haired man looks over his shoulder. "Sure. Whatever."

He looks back at me. "Well, Jaxx with an x, we're going to go for a short hike, and then if your daddy is a good man, he'll come to get you a little later tonight. Does that sound fun?"

"I want my mommy," I cry. "I want to go home."

The man frowns. "Yeah. I'm afraid it will be your daddy and your daddy's home."

I kick out with my feet as the man begins to lift me out of the car. "No! No! Leave me alone!"

"All right, have it your way, Jaxx. I was going to let you hike with us, but you're going to make me carry you over my shoulder."

The dark-haired man lifts me up and drops me on his shoulder. It squishes my tummy and makes it hard to breathe. As he shuts the car door, I see Winnie and cry out for him.

"Oh, for Pete's sake. Grab that stupid bear for the kid, Chester."

All I see as the man carries me are leaves and the back of the dark-haired man's boots. It's getting harder and harder to breathe, and I miss Mommy and Aunt Tracy. I just want to go home.

"Leonard, are you sure about this?"

"The time to talk was before we took the job from Nolin."

"But what if you're right. What if, because of what happened, Stephen decides not to pay us?"

"I'd say he has four to five days to reconsider. If he loves his kid, he will pay us and take his chances on the run. If he doesn't, it's not my problem."

"But he is just a little kid."

"No! He is a job. Just a job."

My tummy hurts from being on the man's shoulder. We seem to walk forever, and I just want to stop. Then we finally do. He sets me down on a dirt floor, and as the air comes back into me, I see that I'm in some sort of hole. I don't like it in here. It smells old, and there are spiders in the corner.

"I want to go home."

The dark-haired man stares angrily down at me. "Well, this just won't do, Jaxx. I can't have you making a big commotion letting people know where you're at." He pulls at my legs, making me fall from my seated position. Leonard takes one of my tennis shoes off and then my sock. "It's your own fault, kid. If you had been braver, I could trust you to stay quiet. But you made me do this."

I don't understand what he is talking about. But he pulls my chin down with one hand as he starts to shove my sock in my mouth. I move my head from side to side. But he pushes harder, and I can't stop him because he is so much bigger than me.

I don't understand. I don't know what I did wrong.

"Leonard..."

"Don't even start, Chester. We would already be getting paid if you had done your job."

The door closes. The hole I'm in is so dark I can't see anything. My mouth hurts from the sock holding it open, and I can feel the spiders looking at me from the corner, waiting to come to eat me, and I can't do anything about it.

A firecracker explodes outside of my hole. I flinch and pee myself.

I just want to go home.

I've quit crying because I need to be brave. Mommy will come to get me. She always has, and I know she will today. I just wish she would hurry.

There's a rumbling sound that shakes the earth. I stop breathing as I wonder what it is.

A tap-tap-tap begins to beat on the roof of my hole. Drops of water strike my face.

I wipe the rain from my face and realize I am sprawled on the driveway next to Chase's truck. As I comprehend that my "gifts" have given me a clue, the excitement builds in me.

I can help Jaxx.

This is what Dionis wanted.

Scrambling to my feet, I close the truck doors and run into the house. I take the flight of stairs to Chase's room and crash through his door as I flick on the light.

"Chase!"

"What the devil!" He rolls to the side of his bed and stops when he recognizes me. "What are you doing, April?"

"I know where Jaxx is!"

He opens his mouth and then closes it with a frown.

"I had a vision. It's so awesome. I saw everything."

Chase sits up and scratches the back of his head. "A vision?"

"Yes." I lift the amulet from my chest. "Dionis brought the amulet back to me after I threw it in the lake, and when she made me check your truck, I had the vision."

"Dionis?"

"What is all the ruckus about?" Dusty asks from the doorway.

Chase shakes his head. "Honestly, I haven't a clue."

I turn to Dusty. He will understand. "I had a vision, Dusty. I know where Jaxx is."

Dusty frowns as he pulls at the red whiskers under his chin. "Alright."

I look back and forth at them. "We need to go. *Now!*"

Chase looks at his phone. "It's 3:35 a.m., April. Where do you want us to go?”

"Back to that old house in the woods. Jaxx is in that cellar. I know it."

"April, we searched the cellar."

"There has to be a secret door or something."

"What is she talking about, Chase?"

He exhales. "We found this old house, and it had a potato cellar. But there is nothing down there except some old mason jars that the raccoons and rats had turned over. No kid."

"Then it's another house!"

"April, what other house?" Chase asks.

"I don't know. Jaxx is out there in a cellar, and we're wasting time. They shoved a sock in his mouth, and he is having difficulty breathing."

"Who did?" Chase asks.

"Leonard and Chester."

"Who?" Dusty asks.

"Aren't y'all listening to anything I'm saying?"

"I'm trying to," Chase says. "But I do not understand any of it."

"Fine. If you won't help, I'll do it myself."

Chase points as I turn from him. "Catch her!"

Dusty collects me up in a bear hug as I try to pass by him.

"Let me go!"

"Stop it," he growls. "We didn't say we wouldn't help. But you're going to take the time to bring us up to speed, and we will be prepared with a plan."

"But he is out there all alone and scared!"

"You won't do him any good if you rush out there and get lost or break an ankle."

The April side of me understands that Dusty is correct. Still, the visceral fear I felt from Jaxx's experience remains strong and is hard for me to quell. "You promise?"

Chase comes up alongside us. "April ... we want to bring him home as much as you do. But we're going to do this right."

"Yes. Deliberate and with a plan."

I know my brothers are correct, and I trust their counsel implicitly. Still, I don't believe Jaxx has time for an organized plan.

Chapter 20

Dusty herds me toward the kitchen. I understand that my brothers want to move forward in their usual deliberate, methodical manner. Unfortunately, I don't believe we have the luxury of time on our side.

No. I do not still have an umbilical cord tied to Jaxx. I do not feel his current plight, or if he is alive at all. Still, given when Jaxx was abducted and the condition he was left in, we are fast approaching the end of his opportunity for survival. We don't have time to sit around the kitchen table and discuss plans.

"Dusty, I really don't think we have time. We need to leave now."

"Are you confident enough to identify where he is from your dream?"

I bite my lip as we turn into the kitchen.

"Because if you had *that* level of clarity with your vision, I would've expected you to say exactly where he was, not that we had to search."

Dusty the writer. Always cognizant of syntax. As he often says, "Say what you mean and mean what you say because words count."

He grasps the refrigerator door handle and looks at me pointedly. "Well?"

"No," I grouse.

"It's pitch-dark out there anyway. Even with the lanterns, it would be difficult searching in the woods," Chase adds.

I draw in a shaky breath and try to square my brothers' practical logic with the emotional time clock ticking in my heart. This is truly taking on a darned if we do, darned if we don't-like conundrum appearance.

If we do it my way, run out of this house like our hair is on fire and drive like demons to search the woods in the dark, we're liable to fall into an abandoned well and break a leg or worse. Still, as we sit here planning Jaxx's rescue, he may be taking his last breath of life. Recovering a little boy's body after he dies seems like a Pyrrhic victory.

"Fine. But can we make it quick?"

Dusty cracks eggs into a glass bowl as Chase turns on the coffee maker. "I'm waiting on you, darlin'. Tell me what you saw," Dusty says.

Chase peeks nervously over his shoulder as he pulls water bottles from the refrigerator. I'm as uncomfortable talking about the supernatural in front of Chase as he is listening to it. We'll both have to get over our aversions for the sake of time.

"In the vision, I was Jaxx during his abduction."

Dusty's eyebrows lower as he pushes his cheek out with his tongue in thought.

"It's not as clear as I would hope." I release a frustrated breath.

"How so?"

"Understand, I wasn't there; I was Jaxx. I was seeing everything through his eyes. Everything in my mind was being processed as if I were a five-year-old. I was experiencing the events as a little boy."

Dusty's upper lip draws back as he stares at me.

"That's messed up," Chase whispers as he stops packing our backpacks.

I lick my lips. "I know. Right?"

"Okay, in the interest of time, we will have to table that for later. It might be something to talk to Granny or Nana about. Let's cut to the important. Where are we going?" Dusty asks as he pours the scrambled eggs into the Teflon-coated skillet.

"It has to be close to where we looked the other day."

"Chase, I thought you said that y'all combed through that place?"

"We did. We walked grid half a mile into the woods before we heard April hollering that she had found Jaxx's bear and the old house. We had seventy folks looking in every nook and cranny of that wreck. That is the only reason we found the potato cellar."

I point at Chase. "That's it. They put Jaxx inside of that cellar."

Chase shakes his head slowly. "Nah. I searched every inch of that cellar. Twice. I knew that was the best place to hide him if he were in that structure."

"There has to be like—I don't know—a secret trapdoor or fake wall down there."

"It's dirt." Chase pushes his chest out as he rolls his hands palms up. "How you gonna put a secret door in dirt?"

"Yeah, I'm not buying the Narnia bit either. It seems a bit far-fetched."

I lace my hands behind my head. "Bless it! I don't know. This is so frustrating."

"You ought to try being on this side of the discussion," Chase says as he returns to packing our provisions.

"Not helpful, Chase," Dusty says as he slides the tray of toast into the oven.

"No, it's okay. You're right. It can't be easy to have a freak for a sister."

Chase pivots, placing his hands on his hips as he glares at me. "Really? I don't think we have time for a pretty princess pity party."

Some days I really hate Chase as much as I love him.

"Egg sandwiches are almost ready," Dusty says to defuse our stare down.

"I'm gonna call Buzz first and have him get together as many people as possible to meet up at the clearing."

I'm suddenly filled with panic. "No, don't."

"Why?" my brothers say in unison.

I stroke the violet amulet on my chest as I think. It's only a gut feeling, and if I'm wrong, it will cost Jaxx his last chance. But maybe Granny is right. Perhaps I should embrace and trust my powers. Or, at least this one time, get some good out of my "gifts." Today, now, I should embrace them. Even if I turn my back on them forever after Jaxx is safe.

"What if having so many people there the other day kept me from sensing Jaxx's presence?"

"Is that a thing?" Chase asks.

"Yeah, is it?" Dusty asks.

I shrug. "How am I supposed to know? All I know is that it didn't work the other day." I lift the amulet. "And I didn't have this the last time we searched. It might help, and I prefer not to have to explain it."

Chase crosses his arms. "Yeah, that pulsating purple disco look is a bit odd. I won't call Buzz."

Fudge! I forgot. "No, do call him."

"Geez, you can try the patience of a saint. Which is it?"

"I'm sorry. I just remembered what Jaxx saw— I know who kidnapped him, remember?"

Both brothers favor me with an intense stare. I have their full attention.

"One was named Chester." I cover my lips with my hand. "He had a really full, bushy, blond mustache, and his nose was red and bulbous, like maybe he drank too much."

"Last name?" Dusty asks.

I cock my head. "Dude. I was a five-year-old."

"Fair."

"The other, his name was Leonard. He was the mean one. I think he was the one that worked up the deal with Stephen."

"Stephen was involved from the start." Chase's eyes narrow into slits. "How could he?"

"At least in the vision I had. Leonard kept saying that Nolin wouldn't pay them because they had killed his—oh man. They killed Gemma, but they weren't supposed to. They were supposed to get Jaxx and bring him to Stephen. But somehow,

Gemma got killed, which threw the plan into a tailspin. I remember they were arguing and…" I put my head in my hands.

"April," Dusty says softly.

I look up and exhale. "They left that little boy out there to die."

Dusty raises his eyebrows and nods slightly.

"How can they do that?"

"Evil is as evil does."

I look at Chase as tears well in my eyes.

"Don't try to understand it, April. Can you tell us anything else about Leonard? If the police can locate those two men, they can be extracting Jaxx's exact location while we search the house you found the other day. To save time."

"Yeah, save time," I repeat as the brevity of the situation and the callousness of the men's act of self-preservation against a defenseless child settles on my heart. I feel tiny fissures break open my spirit as darkness envelops me.

Dusty opens the oven and pulls out the tray of toast. His motion brings me out of my own mind and back to the task at hand.

"Leonard has raven-black hair and piercing blue eyes. They both have the same eyes. Maybe they're related."

"Okay. That's good. Anything else?"

The smell memory comes back to me, of being in the car. "Yes, we were in a four-door sedan. And one of them smokes heavily. The car reeked of cigarette smoke."

Chase nods eagerly. "Good. As many different variables as we can get, the better. It will help jog someone's memory of who these characters might be if they are local. Understand, I believe that Jaxx is close to where we looked the other day. It's the logical conclusion between his father being killed there and you finding his Winnie-the-Pooh bear. Unless those turkeys cooked up some elaborate hoax to lead Stephen to a wrong location."

"Do you really believe that?" I ask.

"No more than your magical door in a dirt wall," Chase smirks.

Chapter 21

At my urging, as soon as Chase parks the truck, despite the poor lighting conditions, we make a beeline into the woods to search the cabin. The sun is narrowly cresting the horizon as we reach the house. Unlike the earlier search, the temperature is already climbing.

The back of my shirt is soaked in sweat. A combination of early morning Alabama humidity, exertion, and nerves. I pull my wet hair off my neck and wish I had thought to bring a hair tie.

Chase approaches the front door of the dilapidated house and kicks at the top board that remains on the front stoop. It shatters against his boot, and he taps the last of the jagged edges away. He doesn't say a word as he braces against the door and pulls himself inside.

"The potato cellar door is on the kitchen floor," I say to Dusty.

He nods his head as he pulls his phone out of his pocket.

"There is no service up here."

"I see that. I was hoping to be able to use GPS to figure out exactly where we are. It seems like we're close to Chief Joe's property."

I point down the hill. "The lake is right there. Chief Joe's property is not anywhere near the lake."

Dusty crosses his arms. "Yeah. I suppose you're right."

"I'm going in to see if anything looks different today. Are you coming?" I notice his expression as he eyes the dry rot-riddled stair Chase kicked away. "The floor seems to be in decent shape except for where the tree is growing."

"Oh, I'm not worried about that."

It's best not to call Dusty on his fib. I can't blame him for being concerned if the old floor will hold his weight.

"Check around the foundation for clues if you don't mind," I say as I stretch my leg up to the doorway and pull myself into the foul-smelling house.

"My pleasure."

I walk to where Chase left the potato cellar open from the other day. To his point, if Jaxx was in a dark place, this couldn't possibly be it. Unless maybe Stephen moved him from the potato cellar somewhere else.

But then Jaxx would have been with his dad when the police had the shootout with Stephen.

I peer down into the cellar and swing my lantern side to side. My light illuminates the back half while Chase's lantern lights the far end of the smallish room.

"April?"

"Yes."

"Come on down here. Watch your step on that ladder; it's a little wobbly."

I climb down the ladder into the earthen room. The scent of red clay mixes with the faint odor of vinegar and spoiled vegetables.

Chase holds his lantern up toward me. "I didn't want you to think I was making fun of you. You weren't down here the other day, and I want you to see that what is in the cellar is smooth dirt. There is no place for a door, and I've even checked the floor. There is not like a second trapdoor."

"I believe you."

He rolls his eyes. "I'm not asking you to believe me. I'm asking you to put a second set of eyes on it and make sure that I'm not missing anything."

I do as Chase requests and make a slow circuit of the room, deliberately checking every inch of the earthen wall and floor. While I do, the amulet vibrates ever so slightly, and I capture residual emotions without reaching out for them.

Suddenly self-conscious, I turn to my brother. Chase is sitting on one of the overturned shelves, watching me patiently.

Slowly, I lower the defenses in my mind, and the emotions flow freely over the top. They are not just from the cellar. The entire home has the signature of quiet desperation, and I reach out further, believing that it could be Jaxx's as he nears the end.

"Chase?" Dusty's voice rings out through the house.

"Down here," Chase replies.

"Come here."

Chase shakes his head. "I don't know who died and made that boy king." He moves toward the ladder. "Will you be okay down here by yourself?"

I nod my head and wave for him to go on. It's best anyway. I'm barely picking up the voice, and Chase is distracting me.

The amulet intensifies its glow and vibration as it warms against my sternum. An inaudible voice echoes in my mind. Desperate for any clue where Jaxx might be, I lean forward into the humming and drop the rest of my defenses.

The volume of the chatter increases, but I still cannot make out the words. I close my eyes to focus more fully. Perhaps, if it's not Jaxx, I'm picking up Leonard and Chester's conversation. That will surely give me a solid clue where to find Jaxx.

I cross my arms as the cellar is significantly colder than outdoors, and my damp T-shirt is now working against me. A small amount of discomfort for me to bear to bring Gemma's son home safely.

"Not my 'maters."

Slowly, I'm dialing in on the chatter in my mind. The residual of Leonard and Chester's conversation is coming to me. It makes all the sense in the world, considering the two men who had unintentionally killed a woman while kidnapping her son must have had a high degree of emotion during their discussion.

"I sed, not my 'maters!"

Oddest thing ever. That can't be what they were talking about. I open my eyes and frown as I try to think.

If not for the slow undulation of the black cloud in the far left-hand corner, I would not have noticed it. I take a step backward and feel for the ladder.

The black cloud floats forward along the floor beams above.

Large puffs of frozen vapor plume from my mouth as I pant. I reach back and jam my fingers on the wooden ladder rung, driving a splinter into my hand.

The cloud columns down two feet from the cedar beam above, and shadowed, gray eyes appear within its swirling, black mass. *"Did you hear me, girl? I sed not my 'maters. Now git!"*

I'm not sure if I scrambled up the ladder or simply jumped eight feet up and landed on the kitchen floor. All I know is one second, I'm at the bottom of the potato cellar, and the next, I'm slamming the potato cellar door shut.

The thud of the heavy door thumping closed rocks the unstable structure, and the floor shifts under my feet as dust powders up from the hardwood slats. Birds take flight from the cedar tree in the center of the house.

"April? Are you all right?"

I put the counter to my back and glare at the closed cellar door, praying I do not see black wisps of smoke creep up through the edges. "I'm good."

"What was that noise?" Chase asks as he comes into the kitchen.

I point at the cellar door. "I figured I'd close it, and it got away from me."

He nods his head. "Uh-huh."

"I think I'm going to take another look around outside."

"Okay. Are you sure you're all right?"

"Right as rain."

"Listen, Dusty thinks that one of us should go back to the clearing where we can get phone service and check if Buzz had any luck finding those kidnappers. So, I will head back since I can make it quicker than him. I also asked Buzz to check the county tax plat map to see if there are any other houses nearby. Just in case."

"That's good thinking," I say as we step outside.

"Yeah, even a blind squirrel finds a nut every now and then." His mirth turns to concern when I don't laugh. "Are you sure you're fine?"

"Positive." I am positive that though I like a good tomato, I may never eat another one again.

While Chase goes to get word from the outside world, Dusty and I continue our search around the outside of the house, in my case to avoid the cellar. We might as well be a couple of blind squirrels, minus the lucky nuts.

The longer this goes on, I realize why Chase was so adamant this morning that there was nothing up here. The structure is tiny, and with seventy people the other day, we probably examined every inch of the property in an hour.

The sun has crept up, driving the temperature easily above ninety degrees to worsen matters. It's like being inside a tropical sauna, and I can feel the steam coming up from the wet leaves as sweat trickles freely down my spine.

"Where did you say you found the stuffed bear?" Dusty asks me for like the third time.

I point in the direction of the clearing. "About a hundred yards in that direction."

"Do you think we should walk back up there and maybe make another search? Just to make sure we didn't miss something? Maybe there is an old well or a barn in that direction."

My earlier concern is slowly turning into sorrow. Even though I don't want to, I think little by little, I'm coming to the acceptance that if we do find Jaxx, he won't be alive. I'm out of ideas, and today my "gifts" have been nothing but trouble. In fact, I'm not even sure that the vision I had of Jaxx was accurate anymore.

Still, I must hope and pray that the dream was accurate enough to identify the kidnappers. Maybe I had the location wrong. Perhaps it was because we were in these woods the other day, and the site stuck in my mind when Jaxx is in another forest altogether. But at least if we got the names of the abductors correct and if they're local, the police will have some luck and be able to find out where they put Jaxx. I know it's a long shot, but at the moment, a long shot is better than no shot.

"Sure, it can't hurt."

Dusty's face is almost as red as his hair. "Do you feel like you need to take a break?"

"Maybe in a minute. But I want to check out that area around the bear first. It makes more sense that it was dropped close to where they put Jaxx."

"I'm not sure what makes sense to me anymore."

"No. Don't do that. Only positive thoughts."

I exhale. "Yes, sir," I say sarcastically.

Dusty chuckles. "There is that April we all know and love."

I don't bother to respond as I look to the left, wishing that I will find an additional clue like the one I found the other day.

How quickly someone's life can turn on a dime. Gemma had built a remarkable life for Jaxx and Tracy. It sounds like they had a lovely support nucleus. And then Stephen decided to ruin it for everyone. I bet he didn't care about Jaxx, if I were to guess. Stephen just wanted to lash out at Gemma.

Stop it, April. You lost the right to hypothesize about the relationship when you checked out of being her friend.

True. I would've warned Gemma about Stephen. But then again, there would be no Jaxx without Stephen, and she gave her life trying to protect her son.

I stop and rub my forehead. Life is so complicated how things are all intertwined. Some days you can't remove the bad without destroying some of the good.

Chase is walking up the path toward us. The promise of good news from Buzz and the police officers energizes me, and I jog toward him.

His facial features come into focus, and I smile.

Our eyes meet, and he shakes his head. I stop running.

Chapter 22

I stand still as Chase approaches us. I can't bring myself to ask him.

"I'm so sorry, April."

"I suppose it was a Hail Mary from the get-go."

He nods his head slowly. "I suppose. But it's always worth a try. You never know when you might get lucky."

"Not today," I whisper.

"No. It doesn't appear so."

"What did you find out?" Dusty asks as he makes his way to us.

"Do you want the incredibly odd or the unbelievably bad run of luck first?"

Dusty shakes his head. "If neither one is helpful, it doesn't matter. Just tell me."

Chase points back up the trail. "For the weird part, according to the tax records, that house doesn't exist."

"How does that happen?"

"I'm not sure. It could be that land reverted to the county for tax liens, and because the structure was in such poor condition, it wasn't recorded. The important thing is that nothing else was built along this trail. I figured that. If there were, surely the county would've laid down a little bit of asphalt sometime over the last sixty years."

"I'm guessing nobody knew who Leonard and Chester were,"

Dusty says.

Chase shakes his head. "Oh no, they're quite famous over in Arab. Or should I say infamous?"

"Were they able to get anything from them when they talked to them?"

"Well, they're not in a real talkative mood right now. It seems somebody paid them a visit and put some brass through the cousins' heads."

Dusty drops to a squatting position and puts his head in his hands. "Aww, no. Stephen?"

"They were shot with a 9mm, which is what Stephen was carrying when he shot it out with the cops. But they won't know anything until the ballistics come back. 9mm pistols are as common as mosquitoes."

"Then that is that. Everybody who knew or might know where Jaxx is being kept is gone."

"I'm afraid so."

I turn and walk away from my brothers. There is nothing to say anyway.

If I were to sit and talk with them, they would tell me how the important thing was that we tried. They would point out all the extra effort we spent attempting to help the authorities find Jaxx.

But it doesn't change anything. We lost. And lost spectacularly.

I despise losing. But as much as I hate losing, I've never felt so hollow after getting my butt kicked as right now. Because not only did I lose, but a little boy is waiting somewhere for his mom, aunt, or me to save him from the dark hole before the spiders eat him or he dies of dehydration. How could I let him down?

Mindlessly, I step up into the house and stare at the cedar coming through the ceiling. Why did I think that his kidnappers would hide him in this pile of garbage?

What did the cousins tell Stephen? Did Stephen not make it up the trail before the police showed up? Or did he come out here, and he couldn't find Jaxx either.

Warily I stare at the cellar door. I need to mention to Dusty that he should get his paranormal team out here to examine it since there is an active spirit in the cellar. I don't believe it is strong enough for them to record with their equipment. I believe the power of the amulet is what allowed the spirit to appear.

I open the side door of the kitchen. It leads out to the opposite side of the house. The sun shines on this side, keeping the dry rot at bay. I sit and stare at the lake hundreds of yards down to my left.

A blue jay calls out from high above. It is followed by a mockingbird's mimic as it flies low and lands close to a honeysuckle bush to my left, a hundred yards out.

Crossing my arms on top of my legs, I tuck my head onto my arms. I hurt so bad, and the tears fall.

"Hey, there is no crying at the lake."

I don't look up at Dusty as he sits next to me. Something cold touches my arm.

"Drink this water. You need to hydrate."

I tilt my head as I take the water from him. "Jaxx needs to hydrate. He hasn't had water in three days."

Dusty holds my gaze as he nods. "We're out of cards to play. What are you gonna do?"

"It isn't fair, Dusty."

"I'm not gonna argue that point with you." He sighs. "But when it's all said and done, we will have to dust ourselves off and start over again. We'll do the best we can and move on."

"I felt his fear. I mean, I really felt it."

"I believe you. I also believe I can imagine that fear without having your abilities."

I blow a breath of air rudely through my lips. "Abilities, my butt. All they were today was a distraction. Not one iota of help."

"Now, come on. If Stephen had not become trigger-happy, we could have found Jaxx's location from the cousins today. And likewise, if Stephen had not been a bonehead and shot it out with the police, *he* could tell us."

"And if Stephen had been a decent dad, he would not have hired the cousins to take Jaxx."

"And then there is that."

I've quit crying, thankfully. But my sadness has been replaced with anger, and I'm as irritable as a wet hornet. "I guess I should head back to school. I have a lot going on the next few weeks."

"That's right. You get your big, bad JD card punched."

"That is the idea."

"Just keep your eye on the prize, April. That is all you can do."

"I suppose."

Dusty squints and leans forward. "Do you see that?"

I attempt to follow his line of sight. It is in the direction of the honeysuckle bush.

"What is that?" He points to the left of the honeysuckle as he stands.

There is a profile only a few inches above the scrub grass in the area. A swarm of black horseflies circle over it.

Chapter 23

Dusty stands and lumbers quickly down toward the swarm of flies. I stare in disbelief and loathe the idea of following him.

He has obviously forgotten that we're searching for a missing child. The last thing I want to see is something that resembles a body in the grass with a squadron of horseflies above it.

I just can't. What was supposed to be a simple favor for Chase has turned into a personal nightmare.

If we found Jaxx and he is dead—and worse, he was out here the other day, and we missed him by the length of a football field —I will crack.

I've become too vested in this search for it to end in this manner. Maybe I'm different than other people, or perhaps it's because he is not my child, but if Jaxx is not alive, I would much rather someone else find him after I leave town. No, to see him dead in scrub grass after lying in the heat and rain for three days. I just can't.

Dusty circles around the vast honeysuckle bush and stops. He braces both hands on his hips and stares at the object.

So many emotions run through me at the same time that I can't tell if I'm cold, about to break into a sweat, or about to vomit. Basically, I feel how I felt the last time I got food poisoning. I know it wasn't from the egg sandwich this morning.

He continues to stare down as he shakes his head. Still, I don't want to know. I think to get up and walk back to the truck so that I don't have to learn the truth.

"This just burns me up."

His tone is angry, but that is not how I expect him to sound if we located Jaxx. Tentatively, I allow myself to breathe a sigh of relief.

Dusty turns in my direction as he flails his right arm. "How long has deer season been over?"

Odd question. Plus, Dusty should know better than me, since he still goes a couple times each year with Chase. "Twelve weeks," I say.

He points at the object on the ground. "This happened this week."

A shiver runs up my backbone as I realize what we're discussing and put it together with the dream that brought me home this weekend. I swallow hard as I pull myself up. I shuffle my moccasins through the shin-high grass as I walk to where my brother stands.

"The part that really chaps my butt is if you're gonna break the law, at least don't let the animal go to waste. This is just disrespectful."

I come up alongside Dusty and look down at the doe. The exit wound on the right side of her rib cage is already teeming with maggots.

Dusty armbars me. "You don't want to see this, April."

Usually, he would be right. But after seeing it tens of times in my dreams, it no longer triggers my gag reflex.

It is all so similar. Yet not.

In my dream, the deer was on the path. Not in scrub grass.

Also, while quite active and plentiful, the maggots are still in the larva stage and have not moved into the pupa, where they were so prominent in all my dreams.

More importantly, and thankfully, the deer's eyes are shut. And she is not talking to me.

"What kinda idiots target practice on a deer and then leave it to spoil?"

It's a rhetorical question by Dusty. My brothers are avid rule-followers who have difficulty comprehending that few are so fastidious about the law.

A stream of flies crawls from the nostril of the doe. They fly in a straight line away from us toward the lake. The swarming cloud above the deer turns and follows the leading insects toward the lake in single file, forming a long black whip.

As the last of the flies leave the doe, she raises her head off the ground and turns her muzzle toward me. Her large black eyes open wide, blinking twice. Her velvet lips move as she says, "To those that much is given, much is expected."

I grab Dusty's forearm to keep from falling over.

Chapter 24

"Are you all right?"

I shake my head and take another look at the doe. The flies have returned, and her eyes are closed. Only her words remain in my mind.

I pat Dusty on the arm. "Sorry. I lost my balance for a moment."

"I get it. It's a nasty gunshot wound, and she has been out here a while."

The word gunshot sticks in my mind. For some reason, there is something significant about it. I press the heel of my wrist to my forehead as if I can push the relevance out.

Think, April. Why does the familiar refrain the deer said seem to mean something in this instance?

Bless it! Given my paranormal "gifts," this could be completely random. Another red herring. The next thing I know, I'll have an armadillo telling me "to live on less than I earn." Or a squirrel saying, "Turn that frown upside down."

My entire life, everyone has poured some bit of wisdom into my brain in twenty words or less. So why wouldn't a dead deer be talking to me with its own golden nugget of wisdom?

None of this is helpful.

I take a few steps away from the rotting carcass and walk down the slope toward the lake, plopping down in the grass.

At least it wasn't Jaxx. That much I can be thankful for. If I were to find Jaxx's body, I don't believe I could ever unsee it.

As it is, I'm having a terrible time squaring the reality that I will never see Gemma again. I don't believe we are wired to deal with our own mortality in our twenties.

True, before this event, I've been home at least twenty times and never thought to swing by and check in on her. But there always seems to be time.

I really wanted to do this for her. To find her son and bring him home safely to his aunt so they might pick up the pieces and try to move on. But I'm a failure because I can't figure out how to read my visions if they are meaningful.

To those that much is given, much is expected, indeed. What have I been given? A bunch of distracting images and voices that make it appear like I'm in some messed-up version of Alice in Wonderland, overlaid across a professional law career? Hardly helpful.

Definitely not helpful for Jaxx, at least.

For the first time since this morning, I replay last night's dream in my mind. I still feel the fear that gripped my heart when I thought I would suffocate under the blanket. The bruises against my stomach and hips still hurt from when Leonard carried me to the dark hole in the ground. I cringe at the thought of the nasty spiders in the corner that couldn't wait to jump on me and suck my eyeballs out. And then the embarrassment of peeing myself when I heard the firecracker go off.

I stare out over the lake. I can barely see the bridge crossing over to Gunter Avenue from the north side of Highway 79. It would be a hot but gorgeous Alabama day if I was doing anything other than searching for Jaxx.

I unscrew the cap from my water bottle and take another sip as I replay this weekend's events in my mind.

"April?"

Without looking back at Dusty, I put a hand up and wave.

"Okay, I'll give you a minute."

That is best. I'm not positive I can talk right now, and if I were to try, I'm afraid I would break down and start sobbing. I prefer not to cry in front of my brothers. First, because it's embarrassing, and second, neither handles it very well.

Fudge. One sip of water and it went straight through me. I feel like I might have to pee. I prefer not to pee in the woods, but I never know if I can hold it until we get home.

I frown as I look back over the lake. It's spring break, and this area is extremely isolated. Where would the firecracker have come from that caused Jaxx to pee himself?

Turning my shoulder, I look back toward the deer. From this vantage point, the honeysuckle bush has an edge to it.

It wasn't a firecracker.

Dusty is halfway back to the house, and I scream at him, "Dusty, get Chase!"

Chapter 25

I fall to my knees twice as my moccasins slide from under me while scrambling up the hill. I pass by the dead doe, her stench rising in the hot, humid air.

My newfound epiphany shatters as I approach the honeysuckle bush. The hard angle I thought I saw from below disappears. Standing directly in front of the honeysuckle, it has a familiar chaotic shape. Albeit, I have never seen a honeysuckle bush of this magnitude. It is a spectacular specimen, easily ten feet tall and twenty feet wide. The delicate scent of its spicy-sweet blooms makes me smile as it reminds me of pleasant memories on Granny's farm.

This makes no sense; it's March. I focus on what I see rather than the smell, realizing there are no blooms.

The brilliance of the sun dulls. I curl my shoulders inward as I cross my arms, warding off the sudden chill.

Too late, I realize what is happening. Looking behind me, I mark the trail of inky black smoke snaking its way across the grass toward me. I want to yell out for my brothers, but my mouth is paralyzed, as are my feet.

I watch the smoke gather around my shins in my paralyzed state. Shivering as it collects and builds into a column standing before me in a monochrome version of a wiry thin man in coveralls with no shirt.

"I had to build that 'cause of the Commies. Took me the better part of three months, I reckon. I'm still not sure if it will work against them nukes, but I like it better in case of a tornader."

I swallow, and it sounds deafening inside of my head.

A translucent version of the deer appears at the side of the coverall wearing ghost, and the old man scratches the deer between her ears. The doe looks at me, and I swear she smirks.

"I dun told them that ain't no place for children to be playin'. But they wouldn't listen."

The words of the old man penetrate through the fear that is real. Slowly I comprehend what he is telling me so plainly despite the distraction of the paranormal circus in front of me.

"April!"

With Chase's voice, the ghost of the old man and the deer disappear.

Chase does not wait for an explanation of why I called him. He sprints toward me in full-on Captain America mode rushing to my rescue. Dusty lumbers behind him.

"What's the matter!" Chase yells as he approaches.

I turn back toward the honeysuckle bush as I answer him. "There is a bomb shelter somewhere. Jaxx is in it. I run to the right of the bush and flail at the massive plant with my arms. The green foliage separates freely but only exposes a multitude of large corded brown vines under the small delicate leaves. I continue to the top of the hill, separating sections of the bush as I go.

"Here?" Chase asks.

"I think," I say.

It has to be. Why else would the ghost meet me out here? The dead doe, killed by a gunshot, was the "firecracker" that made Jaxx pee. It must be.

Dusty and Chase follow behind me, wrestling the bush apart. As if I missed something, but I don't even mention that to them because maybe I overlooked something in my haste, and they will see it on the second pass.

Desperation builds in my gut as I work my way down the slope on the far side, thickest because of the ample sunlight. This must be it. How could my "gifts" be so cruel as to make me think there is hope again, only to snatch it away from me.

I swear I will do everything possible, never to experience my "gifts" again if they fail me this time. Is it so much to ask that they allow me to bring home a helpless boy?

Please, Lord, make this stupid trait of mine good for something this one time. I'm only asking that they be of value today when they matter the most.

I stop and stare at the two-foot-wide opening. It's a corridor with abundant honeysuckle foliage on either side.

I see the remnants of the eight-foot-tall framed chicken wire fence serving as a blind in front of the concrete block structure to the left.

This must be Jaxx's hiding place. Yet, I'm scared to hope as I walk into the vegetation hallway. I'm frightened that my "gifts" are leading me on to rip away hope one last time and obliterate my faith.

The green door, bubbled with rust pockets, to my left fills me with the excitement of the possibility of finding Jaxx. Simultaneously the dread of what condition he will be in if he is inside dampens my enthusiasm.

"April!"

My throat, suddenly dry again, doesn't work as I attempt to answer my brother. I hold my hand out toward the door but stop inches from touching it. Its metal surface will be full of emotions from everybody from Chester, Leonard, and possibly the last moment of Jaxx's existence.

"Oh, thank goodness. It was like you disappeared into thin air." Chase walks toward me. "Is that a door?"

I nod mutely at him.

"Is it stuck?" He comes up behind me. "Here, let me put a shoulder to it."

I step backward, pushing into the foliage as he moves in front of me. He slams into the door, and it gives way, causing Chase to stumble forward into the shelter.

A dark blanket lies against the far corner of the shelter. We have found Jaxx.

 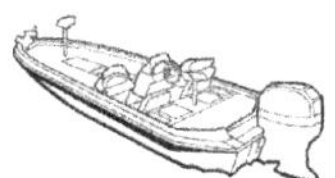 

Chapter 26

Chase catches his balance in one fluid motion and is at Jaxx's side, removing the sock from his mouth. I stand in shock as my brother puts his finger on Jaxx's neck and leans toward the little boy's nose.

"Is he alive?"

Chase turns his heavily lined face toward me. "Yes, but I'm not sure for how long."

"Hey, it's like a plant tunnel," Dusty says at the corridor entrance. He frowns as I look at him. "What?"

"We found Jaxx."

His expression is conflicted. "Oh."

In my periphery, Chase makes to lift Jaxx. "I'm not sure if he will make it, but we have to get him to the clearing to drive him to the hospital as quickly as possible."

With his back to the corner, a translucent child sits at Jaxx's head. His knees are drawn into his chest, and his eyes widen with fear.

I step inside the shelter. "Leave him be."

Chase stops lifting Jaxx. "April, every second counts. He barely has a pulse, and he is dehydrated."

"If you try to move him, he won't survive."

Chase scoffs. "So what? We're gonna let him die in this old shelter?"

Slowly I walk into the small dark room. Jaxx's fear and desperation are heavy in the room. During this dreadful event, the abandoned bomb shelter has become the little boy's purgatory. I fear what it may do to him if he survives. But one thing at a time.

I place my hand on Chase's shoulder. He looks up at me, his expression full of confusion.

"Let me," I whisper.

"Let you what?" Chase asks, his voice cracking.

"Chase. Step away," Dusty says from the doorway.

Chase looks from Dusty to me. "This is nuts," he says as he stands. "He still had a chance," Chase mumbles as he moves toward the door.

I try to control my breathing as I lock eyes with the child ghost and sit down next to him. Once situated with my back against the wall, I gently pull Jaxx into my lap, cupping his head in the crook of my left elbow. I hesitate for the briefest of moments, not knowing how this will affect me, and then move forward, placing my right hand on Jaxx's sternum.

Slowly my hand warms, and I feel my energy ebbing into Jaxx. But still no improvement.

"Please, April. I can carry him out of here," Chase begs.

"Shhh," Dusty says.

My belief falters. This is foolish of me to think it would work. It could have been a one-time anomaly, and even at that, it was only a squirrel.

How stupid am I to gamble Jaxx's final seconds on a skill I've only used once in my life?

Still, I remember it as if it were yesterday. I watched one of the squirrels in our yard munching away happily on an acorn when a red tail hawk slammed into it. I was only a few yards away and immediately jumped up and yelled at the bird. As startled as I was a second earlier, the hawk took to the air and left its prey on the ground.

There is no explanation why, but as I examined the squirrel who was dead but without a visible mark, I placed my hand on it.

I suppose I wanted to feel its fur as I mourned its death.

When I did, my fingers became incredibly hot, and a moment later, the squirrel jumped to life. I could barely snatch my hand back as the ungrateful rodent tried to bite me.

As I hold Jaxx against me, I fear that maybe the squirrel's neck was not broken and he was only temporarily knocked unconscious. Perhaps I only thought I healed him. I close my eyes and curl inward toward Jaxx as my body climbs to an insane temperature, even though I can feel the cold draft in the shelter.

This is the cruelest outcome possible. As my grandmothers requested, I fully believed in my supernatural abilities. Today, they have left me the fool again. It's all too much to bear.

"I'm thirsty."

I look to my right, thinking Jaxx's ghost spoke, but it's no longer present. I look down, and Jaxx moves his cracked lips.

Chapter 27

Leaving Guntersville hospital is a bittersweet moment. Sweet, because we found Jaxx, and according to the doctors, he will make a full physical recovery. With his Aunt Tracy's help, I pray he will also be able to work through the tragedy of losing his mom and the fear of his kidnapping.

I have high hope for him that this will take place, and now that I have met the adult version of Tracy, I am confident that she will be the woman for the job if it can be done. She is every bit as strong of a woman as Gemma. The mom who gave her life trying to protect her son.

It's bitter because I know I have forever lost the opportunity of friendship with a wonderful woman. Someone who could have taught me what is essential in life.

As well as I thought I knew Gemma, I realize now I never really listened to her heart when she spoke. All these years later, I know that like so many of the people I know and love from Guntersville, her roots ran deep. Those roots were important to her, and she was where she wanted to be in life, unlike her friend, who was ready to set sail like dandelion fluff on the first available breeze.

We were different. But I loved Gemma during her season in my life and am sad for the loss.

Given my current schedule, it will be difficult, but I plan to make it to Guntersville for my good friend's funeral. Tracy asked me to say a few words at Gemma's service as one of her earliest friends. I haven't made my mind up if that is the right thing to do. As impressed as I was with her in high school, I know the Gemma I knew was only a shadow of the woman she bloomed into. I don't know how to relate the stories of our youth, so they don't take away from the woman everyone was blessed to know.

If I can figure out the right words and believe I can say them without breaking out into full-fledged sobs and becoming the focus of attention, I have time to tell Tracy yes.

A part of me is still salty that this explosion of supernatural gifts took place because of a favor to Chase. Still, if the dream hadn't come to me while in Tuscaloosa and if Chase hadn't called for the favor, Jaxx would be dead.

And look, for once in my life, my "gifts" proved to be of some value. So there is that.

Face it, Chase didn't exactly get off easy in the whole deal. My brother ended up with a totaled boat and missed the entire bass tournament.

I told him I was sorry that he missed his opportunity to be invited to the Bassmaster Series. He said he didn't mind since we were able to save Jaxx. Knowing Chase, I believe that to be a true statement. But I do wish for his sake that things had gone better. Everybody should be able to reach their goals, even if I don't necessarily understand why he wants to make a living by fishing in tournaments every week.

Highway 69 is not the shortest way to Tuscaloosa. But I take it for alternate reasons. As I reach the west side of the lake, I pull over onto the shoulder.

The gravel crunches under my Keds as I walk back up the road toward the lake. The sun beats down on me, making my hair feel as hot as a skillet as beads of sweat trickle down my spine. My legs are still unsteady from having lifted so much of Jaxx's pain earlier.

Stopping at the lake's edge, I look out toward the center, where the dead pines stand on one of the many islands. My arm strength is not *that* good, but I'll throw well to the island's right to be safe.

I pull the amulet out of my purse. Immediately untold power courses through me, and my mind clamps down, not wanting to do what I came here to accomplish.

A migraine stabs at the back of my neck, and voices swirl in my head. Dionis's voice comes forward and screams one last word. *"No!"*

As I draw back, my hand feels like a bungee cord is attached to it. As I whip my arm forward, it barely moves as if someone is holding it back. I open my hand, and the amulet flies a mere thirty feet before making a pleasing *plunk* in the water.

I stare at the point of entry until my shirt is soaked with sweat.

It wouldn't be too difficult to swim out there and dive for the amulet. It's probably only ten or fifteen feet deep where it sank.

Besides, if I get close to the stone, it will glow. That is mighty handy considering the visibility of the water is only a foot or two.

April, this is your moment of choice. Do you want to be a defense attorney or a witch living in a trailer out in the woods by yourself?

Given the proximity of the amulet, the decision is more complicated than I ever anticipated. Still, I turn and walk back to my car with much reservation over leaving my precious.

I have a busy week ahead of me, and I need to talk to my professors about being absent so I can attend Gemma's funeral.

Epilogue

"So are y'all still an item after your 'meet the parents weekend?'"

Martin laughs. "Stop it."

"Well, inquiring minds want to know. Don't keep me in suspense."

"I seriously don't know why you're making such a big deal about this. But if you must know, because you are forced to live vicariously through my relationships..."

"Ouch, now that is harsh."

He laughs again. "Hey, I'm just tagging you back."

"Fair."

"Seriously, all kidding aside. It went well. Penny's mom was extremely nice, and her dad only tried to castrate me once."

"Only once? Wow, y'all must've really hit it off."

"Hey, what's not to love?"

"Oh sheesh, I didn't know we would go here. Let me put my muck boots on before you start spreading all that bull."

"You're so mean, Snow. I have no idea why I keep you for a friend."

"Because you need an effective study buddy."

"I kept my secret that poorly veiled?"

"Yeah, well. Neither of us is particularly good at hiding our motives."

"True." He gasps. "Oh. Penny has a tutoring session this evening with one of her math clients. Do you want to get together on the real estate law information we were studying?"

Finally, back at my apartment, I get out of my car. "I don't know. I'm quite sure I need to go to the grocery store. When I left, the best I recall, I didn't have anything to eat in my apartment." Except for some Cheetos that are going directly into the garbage can.

"I haven't eaten yet. If we go to dinner, you don't have to grocery shop until tomorrow."

Considering the weekend I experienced and my loathing of

grocery shopping, dinner with a friend sounds like an excellent treat. "Sure. Let's do that."

"Okay. Where do you want to meet?"

"Wait a minute. I think I still have a gift card to Angelo's," I say.

"Oh, I love their lasagna."

I stand at my apartment door and reach into my purse for my billfold. My fingers jam into something hard that immediately warms. As I open my purse wider, my jaw drops, and the stoop in front of my doorway illuminates with an eerie purple haze.

"PEACHES!"

The End

Aprils story continues with

Throw the Bouquet

Don't miss the next April May Snow release date. Join the reader's club now.

www.mscottswanson.com

Have you read the prequels? ***The Gifts Awaken*** stories are the prequel series to the ***Foolish*** novel series of April May Snow.

Click to get your copies today!

The Gifts Awaken Prequel Series

Throw the Amulet

Throw the Bouquet

Throw the Cap

Throw the Dice

Throw the Elbow

Throw the Fastball

Throw the Gauntlet

Throw the Hissy

M. Scott lives outside of Nashville, Tennessee, with his wife and two guard chihuahuas. When he's not writing, he's cooking or taking long walks to smooth out plotlines for the next April May Snow adventure.

Dear Reader,

Thank you for reading April's story. You make her adventures possible. Without you, there would be no point in creating her story.

I encourage you to post a review on Amazon. A favorable critique from you is a powerful way to support authors you enjoy. It allows our books to be found by additional readers, and frankly, motivates us to continue to produce books. This is especially true for your independents.

Once again, thank you for the support. You are the magic that breathes life into these characters.

M. Scott Swanson

The best way to stay in touch is to join the reader's club!

www.mscottswanson.com

Other ways to stay in touch are:

Like on Amazon

Like on Facebook

Like on Goodreads

You can also reach me at mscottswanson@gmail.com.

I hope your life is filled with

magic and LOVE!

Made in the USA
Monee, IL
02 January 2023

24362524R00115